COLLIDESCOPE

GRACE CHETWIN

BRADBURY PRESS
NEW YORK

Copyright © 1990 by Grace Chetwin
All rights reserved. No part of this book may be reproduced or transmitted in any form or by any means, electronic or mechanical, including photocopying, recording, or by any information storage and retrieval system, without permission in writing from the Publisher.

Bradbury Press
An Affiliate of Macmillan, Inc.
866 Third Avenue, New York, NY 10022
Collier Macmillan Canada, Inc.
Printed and bound in the United States of America
First Edition
10 9 8 7 6 5 4 3 2 1

The text of this book is set in Times Roman
Book design by Kimberly M. Hauck

LIBRARY OF CONGRESS CATALOGING-IN-PUBLICATION DATA
Chetwin, Grace.
Collidescope / Grace Chetwin. — 1st ed.
p. cm.
Summary: When his spaceship crashes to earth, a highly advanced alien interferes with the lives of two teenagers living on the island of Manhattan during different centuries.
ISBN 0-02-718316-5
[1. Science fiction. 2. Extraterrestrial beings—Fiction. 3. Time travel—Fiction. 4. New York (N.Y.)—Fiction.] I. Title.
PZ7.C42555Co 1990
[Fic]—dc20 89-38255 CIP AC

GRATEFUL ACKNOWLEDGMENTS and thanks to the Museum of the American Indian, at Broadway & 155th Street, New York, for enrichment and inspiration.

Also to Robert Grumet for the kind and informative consultations on the background for this book. And not least to Al Satoshi, Black Belt Third Dan, and his young students who taught me so much about form—and attitude.

For Claire, with love:
It never gets easier.

Glossary of American Indian terms and ancient place names

Aquehonga Manacknong—Staten Island
auke—land, ground
huskanaw—rites of manhood
Konaande Kongh—village located on Manhattan between what is now Lexington Avenue and Madison Avenue from 98th to 100th Streets
Mahicanituk—the Hudson River
o jik̆ ha dä gé ga—the Atlantic Ocean (Iroquois)
sachem—chief
Saperewack—Marble Hill, Bronx
Sapokanikan—a place situated on the bank of the Hudson River near Gansevoort Street in lower Manhattan
shaman—medicine man, healer
Shatemuc—another name for the Hudson River

Prologue

Emerging from the dark side of Pluto, the tiny alien ship flashed silver in the light of the distant sun. Across the egg-shaped vessel's prow were stenciled neat, red symbols; strange dots and slashes meaningless to Earthlings' eyes. In English, they might read:

*I*ntergalactic *S*ociety for *P*lanetary *C*onservation
H.A.H.N. Patrol Scout Class IX/Pod #6

There was no break in the pod's polished sides, no hatch or porthole. The hollow interior—the cabin—was richly studded with many-colored crystals, some small as a thumbnail; others big as a fist: the ship's instrumentation. Here and there, crystals winked on and off at differing frequencies. Most were dark and unlit, awaiting some signal that would trigger them to their proper tasks.

Amidships, the cabin traced the vessel's ovoid curve. Fore and aft, the walls were flat. The front wall housed three tiers of square boxes, twelve to a row. At first glance, they looked like a bank of screens in a TV store. A closer look would show they were not flat at all, but 3-D projectors, or holographs. *Holoboxes.*

When activated, these holoboxes presented visual data from the ship's scanners: charts, graphs, computer-generated constructs; linear models of rivers, seas, and mountains. These boxes were currently set in *porthole* mode, acting as windows to the outside. All together, they formed a compound eye, giving a 360° sweep of the ship's surroundings.

The cabin's back wall housed a storage panel, with rows of doors like lockers in a gym.

And the pilot?

In the middle of the floor was a platform. On the platform was a giant cylinder, seven feet long with hinged lid: the ship's LSRM—Life-Support and Repair Module. In that cylinder the pilot lay enclosed; in dark blue jumpsuit with high neck and long red sleeves, his head encased in a silver cap connected to the cylinder walls by various tubes and wires. He looked quite dead. His chest never moved in that airtight, mylar-padded cocoon; his eyelids never wavered. There he lay, in stasis, awaiting a signal that would trigger him to life, while the craft sped on, past Neptune, then Uranus, and then Saturn, and in toward Jupiter.

Time passed, registered and calibrated in fractions of light years.

The spotless cabin hummed with noise: clicks, and snicks, and whirrings, as the vessel constantly checked and modified its course around Mars, then in toward the third planet from the sun.

Suddenly, as the craft neared that third planet, crystals

winked on in clusters, filling the cabin with radiance. The LSRM lid slowly lifted. Hahn stirred, opened his eyes, and blinked up at the ceiling. Disengaging himself from the metal cap, he rubbed his shaven head and climbed out onto the floor. He touched a crystal in the cylinder's side, a panel opened at his feet, and the LSRM sank into the floor.

Hahn moved into the newly created space and stretched, spreading his arms wide, pressing his large palms against the cabin ceiling. He was big-boned and tall, with generous features and well-shaped skull. His feet, large also, were encased in dark shoes, like running shoes, that made no sound as he moved to inspect the ship's instrumentation and the flickering monitor wall. He had been activated: now to find out why. Leaving the top boxes on porthole mode, Hahn tapped out a series of rhythmic codes, converting the lower lines to show other data.

Stars gave way to charts and numbers.

Hahn surveyed them in surprise. That third planet out from its sun: the last time he'd swung by looking for signs of significant life—eons ago, local time—its atmosphere had been anaerobic: largely methane and carbon dioxide, allowing none but the most primitive of life forms: simple-celled bacteria. But according to the signals now coming in, between his last visit and this one, the planet had "hiccupped," and reversed itself. Now its atmosphere was predominantly oxygen—aerobic—which could mean . . .

The data was streaming in now. No doubt about it. Things had moved radically since his last patrol. If some more complex being now lived upon that world, he'd find it. He had been programmed to identify all shapes and forms of intelligent life, which was just as well, for of all those he'd found on over one hundred different worlds during his career, very few had been remotely human . . .

Hahn checked the top row of boxes, scanning the space around the ship carefully. Several H.A.H.N.s had gone missing on patrol lately, right across the galaxies. Why and how, ISPYC had yet to determine. So caution was the word. With scouts disappearing, emergent planets were increasingly at risk: unrecorded, and unprotected from alien settlers.

Many member worlds of the Intergalactic Federation were not pleased with the space protection laws. Resented ISPYC's efforts to protect evolving worlds from outside encroachment. Defeated by law, land-hungry systems were working to sabotage ISPYC's patrols by any means, illegal, or even deadly . . .

In view of the disappearances, all scouts were on alert. In the event of sudden attack, evasion was the first course. But if capture seemed inevitable, the scout, sworn never to harm his environment, never to be seized by any force hostile to ISPYC, had one final drastic step.

Hahn glanced up to a panel set high in the curve of the cabin wall. Etched on its glossy surface was what looked like a figure eight lying on its side: symbol of infinity. Behind the panel gleamed a large, dark quartz—his doomsday stone, as he called it. In the final resort, Hahn would tap out the access code—three short, one long, three times—on the seal, and it would release, exposing the stone beneath. A single touch on that crystal would send craft and scout on a one-way trip through space and time—nonstop. Once activated, the command could not be canceled.

Hahn eyed the doomsday stone uncomfortably, sensing the inhibiting factors implanted deep within him. Craft and scout had cost so much; could not easily be replaced. Therefore, these inhibiting factors were designed to prevent any scout from self-destructing unless it was absolutely the last resort.

Hahn turned back to the holoboxes. Scanners had picked up a large number of small communication satellites in orbit above the planet's atmosphere, all of them active.

Passing the one small moon, Hahn set his ship in orbit against the direction of the planet's turn, scanning its night and day side continuously.

Data—in rapid strings of binary code—was stacking up in the computer banks too fast for the holoboxes to handle. Scanning it in visual, human terms took far too long, much as Hahn liked it. He put a finger to a terminal in the left wall and stood, eyes closed, head to one side, as though listening.

That planet was inhabited, all right, by many minds and voices, all of which he could hear and understand simultaneously through his built-in translator. And those people were human! This made Hahn feel glad, as he had felt those other times he'd discovered humans, although he wasn't supposed to feel disposed toward one form more than any other. The fact that he felt glad at all puzzled him highly, for he had not been built to *feel* anything. Perhaps, he thought, it was that he himself was of a humanoid cast.

That world down there—it must have a name. Hahn rapidly scanned the swelling data banks, finding what he sought in many sounds and symbols, some dating back to the earliest history of the planet:

. . . erde . . . eorthe . . . erthe . . . erdha . . . jordh . . . jǫrd . . . aírtha . . . terra . . .

His little craft, emerging from dark to light, and passing over a wide land mass in the northern hemisphere, caught and focused on one overriding local name:

Earth.

HAHN

Hahn glanced wistfully into the boxes. The data banks were almost full; his job was almost done. He had discovered another viable world, and recorded proof of its fitness to be entered into the register of protected planets. Once he beamed the data back to ISPYC, Earth was out-of-bounds to grabby alien settlers. Then, his job done, he'd go back into the LSRM to lie dormant while the ship carried him on to the next star system, light years away.

He shouldn't mind going on again, Hahn told himself. He wasn't made to mind. He was designed as a single patrol scout unit, no more, no less.

Still. All those humans down there, going about their lives, quite unaware of him, of his coming and going. Those other worlds where he'd discovered live thinking beings—he'd had to leave them, too, without meeting one of them face-to-face. Hahn was forbidden to interfere with any newly discovered world lest he change the natural course of its evolution. In fact, ISPYC rules forbade him to make the slightest contact with a member of an alien world, or to reveal his presence in any way. His job was merely to observe and record, make his report, then go on, as he'd done faithfully, obediently, from the moment he'd been activated. But, lately, each discovery of one of those planets was leaving Hahn more and more lonely for company—especially human company. Which was strange, for Hahn wasn't supposed to feel lonely: he'd been programmed to operate alone.

Without thinking, Hahn had edged the ship down into stationary orbit over the land mass below. The United States of America, the data said.

Sprinkles of spring were spreading up into the northern latitudes. Hahn had seen it before on similar planets with frozen polar caps, hot equators, and wobbly axes. In fact, his own homeworld, Telfar, ISPYC's base, was one such. When spring came, the sap rose; warmth returned to the land, and new life emerged into a season of hope and fresh starts: a time when all kinds of miracles might happen beyond the city domes that sealed the people in. Sighing, Hahn nudged his craft slowly up the eastern seaboard, scooping up final coded samples of information.

The United States of America.

United. Hahn liked that word. It spoke of cooperation, a cardinal sign of higher intelligence. Wouldn't be long, he thought, before those people down there got around to joining the Federation. Another generation or so—maybe less—and they'd be manning expeditions into space. One such landing on another planet, even one in their own local system, that's all it would take to earn this world galactic recognition.

Another few hundred years only, and they'd reach intergalactic status for sure.

Hahn zoomed in his roboscope for a view from thirty thousand feet, and caught soft blue mountains, and shining silver rivers flowing toward the sea. Looked more and more like Telfar, Hahn thought. There, also, the dominant intelligent species was human, though it was not Telfar's only form of thinking life. Maybe this was why he lingered, looking, even though now the data banks signaled FULL.

He continued north up the glittering coastline, until he was directly above an island of towers that shone like a stack of tall quartz columns in the sun. Beautiful. Its name? Hahn found it in a blink.

Manhattan.

Like a boat, it floated, with the Hudson to port, and the East River to its starboard side. A crowded boat, with many masts, open to the air. On Telfar these days, cities were sealed under quartz domes, their atmospheres filtered and controlled. Megalopolises, that seemed to Hahn more like insect colonies than human dwellings. Rapt, Hahn gazed into the holoboxes, desire growing within him to transmat down there. How long since people on Telfar had walked down a street feeling the sun and wind directly on their faces? Or the rain falling spontaneously from the sky? He focussed the roboscope on the island's southern sector, on a particularly thick concentration of humans, streaming like a turbulent river through narrow, canyon streets. Eye fixed to the 'scope, Hahn zoomed in more closely yet: three thousand feet, three hundred. Thirty. Still going, he edged the 'scope's viewfinder down between tall buildings into a narrow crevasse deep in late afternoon shadow, knowing and understanding exactly what he saw as if he had been born and bred in that city. Moving the 'scope around, he could pick out quite plainly individual pedestrians crowding the sidewalks, and street signs: Broad Street, Wall Street, Hanover. Primitive wheeled traffic packed the thoroughfares. It was Friday afternoon rush hour, the data said. These humans had finished work for the week, and were set on getting home. Most of them hurried by alone, clutching bags and briefcases. Some, like that man and woman there, walked more slowly, rapt in each other. Even as he watched, they ducked out of sight into a coffee shop. As they disappeared, a woman stopped to gaze into a large, bright shopwindow, clogging the sidewalk; creating a jam.

All those humans, so many of them. So like the ones on Telfar even if the surroundings were more aboriginal. . . .

Hahn was just zooming in for yet a closer look when a bottom row box caught his eye: a 3-D radar grid of the space sector behind him. A bright blip was crossing that grid, heading for his ship. Hahn pressed for porthole mode, maximum resolution. The radar grid vanished, replaced by a view of starry space, and Hahn saw that the blip was a silver pod, just like his own—and it was coming straight at him!

Even as Hahn felt his shock of surprise, he mechanically registered the accompanying surge of adrenalin, and checked the flow back down to normal. He slowed his breathing, calmed himself. All these symptoms were the result of emotion, and emotion was a human trait, stemming from the heart. And he was supposed not to feel but to think, and fast. Another scout pod, here, in his patrol sector? How? And why?

Hahn hailed the approaching pod on ship-to-ship frequency.

No response.

The little craft, still on collision course, was now so close that Hahn could see quite plainly the logo on its nose:

*I*ntergalactic *S*ociety for *P*lanetary *C*onservation
H.A.H.N. Patrol Scout Class IX/Pod #24

Pod #24? That had gone missing a while back in the Andromeda section. How had it gotten here? And why this hostile maneuver? Hahn reached to hail again. At that instant, blue light flashed from the pod's nose and hurtled across the void toward him. A disruptor charge, a bolt of blue death-light!

Hahn activated his own craft's deflector shield and swerved. His ship shuddered as the shot grazed its starboard side. A H.A.H.N. turned against his fellow? *What was going on?*

Hahn spun his ship about to face the oncoming craft, his mind racing.

Orders were, when under attack, especially near an inhabited planet, to take evasive action.

Even as Hahn faced about, a second bolt came at him.

Despite the deflector shield, the shot skinned his craft's thin shell, and the little ship juddered, throwing him against the wall. Evasion was not enough. He must fire a warning shot. Hahn righted himself, steadied his craft, then, fixing pod #24 grid-center, he touched his own deep blue firing crystal. A ball of light cut the dark, hurtled toward the other ship's nose.

Hahn called out in dismay. A hit! How, when he had been at pains to miss the craft? The stricken pod twisted, spun, then began to fall in toward Earth's atmosphere. Hahn watched, horrified. All those people down there! The damage from the crash would be catastrophic! He waited for the other H.A.H.N. to use his doomsday button and disappear, to remove himself from this sector of space and time.

But the disabled pod only continued its deadly dive unchanged toward the atmosphere. Of course! Hahn smacked his brow. If H.A.H.N. #24 was acting like an enemy, he would have been subverted. And ISPYC's fail-safe command, erased. This H.A.H.N. wouldn't care whether he hurt anyone or not.

Minutes now, and that pod would crash down upon those masses.

What to do?

There was only one option: to vaporize the stricken pod, now! Hahn checked his power reserves. Those hits had cost. He cut his shield to boost his drive, and dove after the disabled craft.

He had the falling ship dead-center, was just putting his finger to the firing crystal, when light shot across the space between them, catching him full on. Hahn's pod lurched, sent him sprawling.

Fool! He'd been caught with his shield down! Bank upon bank of warning lights signaled damage all over the cabin but his own built-in sensors already warned his ship's hull was breached, and its stabilizers gone wild. He tried to stand, fell back dizzily, his own inner gyroscopes whirling. The enemy craft was aligning for the kill. No need. Hahn's pod labored under the gathering pull of Earth's gravity. In horror, Hahn realized that the tables were turned: now he, Hahn, was the falling bomb!

He threw an agonized glance to the distant crowds in the holoboxes.

Only minutes now.

There was no way he could stop the dive. Hahn eyed the doomsday stone high in the wall, way out of reach. He struggled to haul himself up, only to fall back again. *What to do?* Blow the ship up? There'd be enormous fallout. Crash intact onto those crowds? Code red code red code red—*think!*

He couldn't stop the crash, couldn't change his course through space . . .

There was just one chance, one way out, maybe. Hahn mustered all his strength, came up onto one elbow. Then he reached with his free arm until his groping fingertips found a white quartz button partway up the wall: the ship's built-in time stone. Were there enough seconds left to pull back through *time?* To find somewhere—*somewhen*—with room to crash without causing harm?

He was so close now; he must be almost within sight of those crowds down there. A meteor, they'd think him; a fireball falling from a clear blue sky.

Well, he must make that fireball disappear!

Hahn tapped in the activation code, thinking of the danger to this world's space/time continuum. One error, and his entrance could disrupt the flow of local space and time significantly. Some choice! That or blowing up all those people, and loosing massive radiation!

He pressed for go.

The moving shapes in the top row boxes began to shimmer, then blur as the ship, falling faster, raced back through time. Where, *when,* was he headed? Would he make it back far enough before the crash?

Hahn slowed for a nanosecond, the merest blink of an eye—enough to see that the skyscrapers had given way to brownstone houses, tenements, and busy streets. And lots of people still. His anxiety deepened. Only seconds now to impact.

He went on again. The ship was bucketing badly. The pressure in the holed cabin was dropping fast; the interior, filling with droplets of mist.

Five seconds left.

Hahn kept his hand firmly on the crystal, his eyes steadfast on the changing scene. He sped back another hundred years, then two, the quickening strobe of days and nights fusing into one gray blur, but when he slowed again to check, there were people still, so many of them, in long skirts, breeches, wigs and plumes. Wooden houses, cobbled streets, horses, carriages.

Four seconds.

The houses grew smaller, rougher, and sparser on the ground.

Would they be gone when he hit?

Three, two . . . one!

The streets vanished, leaving woody hills, a wide tract of

marsh: beside the marsh, rough hide shelters, an open bonfire, and lines of drying pelts flapping in the wind.

The ground rushed up. Darkness. Trees. Reed clumps.

There came a sudden tremendous impact. A flash of light, a deafening hiss of steam. And humans? Hahn wondered urgently, as his head smacked the floor. *Were there humans still?*

FRANKIE

Okay, okay,'' Mr. Ho said. ''One more time.''

Groans came from all sides. The class of ten had been warming up and stretching now for more than an hour. Their faces shone with perspiration and the mirrored wall behind Mr. Ho was misting over. The studio, or Dojang, as that carpeted area was called, was not very big by gymnasium standards, and the ceiling was low. Frankie loved it. It was the only Dojang she had ever known, and Mr. Ho, her only teacher. She loved this time of class when her body had warmed up, when she was breathing hard, pulling in the familiar tang of wintergreen through her nose.

''Stop with the complaining,'' Mr. Ho scolded affably. ''You can never do enough of this work. One day it might save your life. Now: charyut!'' *Attention!* At Mr. Ho's command, the class readied themselves. ''Jhoon bi! Shijak!'' *Ready! Begin!*

At once, the three orderly rows went through their last round of sit-ups, each student in turn counting out the Korean numbers:

"Hana!" *One.*

"Dool!" *Two.*

"Set!" *Three.*

"Net!" *Four . . .*

". . . Yul!" *Ten.* Frankie, counting last, tried not to sound too puffed. A brown belt second Gup, she had the highest ranking there, except for Andy Seviglia, a brown belt first Gup—only one belt down from black. She was also the youngest, a lone sophomore among juniors and seniors, and the only girl.

At Mr. Ho's command, the class scrambled up and adjusted their uniforms, taking care as they did so not to face Mr. Ho or the wall where the flag hung, which would be considered an insult. Rule #16 for the Dojang: *When fixing your uniform or belt do not face your Sabumnim (master) or flag.*

"Charyut."

The class snapped to, faced Mr. Ho, towering over him. Frankie looked past him, to his back reflected in the mirror, and the rows of students beyond. He was so small and compact. The smallest there, save for Frankie. Yet he had such power and command.

"We do Poomse," said Mr. Ho. The ritual patterns of punching and kicking that looked like a formation dance. "Jhoon bi." The class took up ready stance. "Shijak: Hana . . . Dool . . . Set . . ."

The Dojang filled with loud hissing as, at the end of each counted move, the class pushed out their breath in the short, sharp, sibilance that gave them strength, and focus, and stamina.

"Okay," Mr. Ho said, when they were done, "we do some one-step sparring for half an hour. Take the person nearest to you, and rotate until everybody has gone against everybody else. Remember," he reminded them, as he always did before they fought one another, hand to hand, "aim your blows carefully. And just tap where you connect. We don't want anyone hurt, okay?"

Now the class began what looked like a strange and complicated barn dance, changing partners at Mr. Ho's clipped commands. After, they moved on to free-form self-defense. Now they could go from just stepping and kicking and punching to choke holds and throws. Again, Mr. Ho warned them not to strike or throw for real; to fake the blows, or stop them short, the way fencers feinted with foils.

Frankie's first opponent was Andy. Taller than she by a full head, he was built like a wrestler, graceful as a dancer—and deadly.

"Hi, Frankie." Andy smiled down at her.

"Hi." Frankie bowed. *Rule #7: Respect all your senior belts, bow when asking a question.* "You go first?" As senior ranking student, he should.

"Okay."

They took up Joonbi, ready stance, facing each other.

"*Ki*-hap!" With the customary loud yell, Andy let fly a side kick to Frankie's head.

"Pshoo!" Stepping back, Frankie raised her arms, crossing her wrists in a high X-block to ward it off. Andy grabbed an arm, spun her around, and locked her in a choke hold.

And there Frankie stayed, for the longest minute, unable to think of a way out. She felt a quick surge of anger at her helplessness, let it go. *Rule #10: Never lose your temper in the Dojang—especially during sparring . . .* She weighed up possible countermoves, rejected them in turn. Lucky one could stop to think in practice: if this had been a real attack she'd be done for by now.

"Having trouble, Frankie?" With uncanny timing, Mr. Ho appeared beside them. Frankie and Andy broke apart and bowed.

"I can't find a way out, sir."

"Then better not to have gotten in, wouldn't you say?"

"Yes, sir. But Andy—"

"Um. Well, here you are. So undo it."

"But I—"

"Try."

Obediently, Frankie let herself be taken once more, then she tried this move and that to twist or break free, without success. Finally, she gave up, conceding defeat.

Mr. Ho shook his head. "Won't do. Okay, Frankie: what are our three options in karate?"

That was easy: "Evasion, control, immobilization, in that order."

"Meaning?"

"If someone strikes, don't be there. Failing that, go for control."

"Meaning?"

"Meaning, try to reverse the situation: put your attacker on the defensive, passing the initiative to you."

"And failing that?"

"Then you strike. Go for the break—"

"But only if you have to," Mr. Ho said, raising his voice

as the rest of the class came to watch. "Never forget that karate is about self-defense, not attack. This power you're all acquiring: you know it's deadly. So never, never abuse it: that's a sacred trust. Now, as Frankie just said, if trouble hits, don't be there." He looked around at all the lesser belts. "If you can't remove yourself, then you block. Only if this fails may you start to think of breaking arms and legs to save yourself. Got it?" Everybody nodded. "Okay, let's look what we have here. Andy has a lock on Frankie, so she's missed out on evasion. What does she do?"

"Go for control," somebody said.

"Good." Mr. Ho turned to Frankie. "Back into that choke hold. Perhaps you'll think of something now."

Frankie obeyed, placing her feet, letting Andy take her from behind as before. The moment his arms closed around her, Frankie had a new idea. "*Ki*-hap!" Taking a good breath, she pushed it out explosively, thrusting back her heel in a strong axe kick—a score! Andy let go.

Mr. Ho beamed. "See? You found a way! And that's not the only one, by any means. Okay, class, to work. Not you, Frankie," Mr. Ho went on, as the watching students scattered back into their own space, "you're not through."

"Sir?" Frankie was puzzled. "I took control and broke free."

"Only *after* the fact. So try again, and this time don't let Andy get ahold." As Frankie hesitated, at a loss, Mr. Ho wagged a finger. "Stubborn Frankie, sticking with the same old options, even if they get you killed! How many times do I tell you—there's always more than one way out of trouble."

As they took up ready stance once more, Frankie thought

fast. She had to keep her distance, so no arm blocks . . . How else to protect herself and also take control? Oh, dumb, she thought disgustedly, as the answer came. Keep going, of course! Be a moving target! As Andy's foot came around, Frankie dodged, spun and threw a counter kick of her own, sending Andy backward out of reach.

Mr. Ho nodded approval. "There. You see?"

Frankie bowed, scarcely able to hide her jubilation. "Yes, sir."

"Frankie: the first move we think of: it's not necessarily the best or only one. Say after me, *there's always more than one way out of trouble*. Remember that," he said when she had repeated the words, "and we have real power: the power of choice."

Frankie folded her belt, laid it on top of her gear, zippered up her bag and shouldered it. She was the last to leave the locker room, an alcove off what was really a converted store; a long, narrow space, running from front to back of the building. The storefront sign read,

VALLEY STREAM MARTIAL ARTS ACADEMY
TAE KWAN DO KARATE; KUNG FU; SELF DEFENSE
DIRECTOR: KWANG HO

Mr. Ho was at his desk as she crossed the floor.

"Heard from your Dad, Frankie? How's Cape Kennedy?"

"Great, Mr. Ho," she said. "But it's Cape Canaveral." Mr. Ho always got it wrong, and she couldn't ever be sure whether he was teasing.

"Has he launched any rockets lately?"

"The Atlantis goes up next month, sir."

"That's good. Give him my regards," Mr. Ho said, exactly as he had every week of the two years since Dad had left, and added, as always, "You did real well today. Keep it up." He'd never say that in class, of course, Frankie thought, walking on.

She paused for a moment in the shop doorway, pulling up her collar. It was much colder since she'd come here from school. And it was growing dark. She set off for home at a clip, to keep her heated body from getting chilled, and reached the house in record time of under ten minutes.

There was a note on the refrigerator door. Dinner was in the dish marked, dinner. Frankie was to put it in the microwave for eight minutes exactly. She took out the dish, lifted the cover, and sniffed. Last night's cauliflower cheese. She put it back, and, to her relief, found one last slice of pizza in the freezer. *Later*.

She grabbed a soda and ran upstairs to take a shower.

Half an hour after, scrubbed, and tingling, and in fresh clothes, Frankie ambled down into the sitting room. Mom was usually home around this time, being a teacher and all. But this semester she was taking a social studies enrichment program at Hunter College in the city on Fridays. So far, Frankie had enjoyed having the house to herself for an hour or two, but today, she missed Mom being there to welcome her.

Frankie flopped onto the couch and opened up the paper she'd brought in off the front porch. Same old depressing stuff. Twenty more years, the Brazilian rain forests would be gone. The Puerto Rican parrot was almost extinct. And another oil spill was spreading all over. "Doesn't anybody care?" she asked aloud.

Some people did. But not enough. And big business always put money first, Frankie thought angrily. She turned the pages. "Significant event sometime today will change your life," her horoscope said. "Box yourself into a corner, and a superior takes you to task."

"Ha! ha!" As Frankie threw the paper down, the phone rang. Hooray. Anna, to say when they were leaving for the movies. "Hi, old buddy!" she cried into the mouthpiece.

"Frankie?" Not Anna, but Mom, sounding breathless, and up a notch or two. Her posh phone voice. Frankie went on the alert. Who was with her?

"Frankie, did you see the fireball?"

"Fireball?"

"Around five forty-five. Maybe you couldn't see it from Valley Stream. Bingham said—" Her mother broke off. "They said it was a freak storm. Anyway," she went on lamely. "I wondered if you knew."

Frankie's hands pricked. "Mom, what's up?"

"Nothing!" her mother said quickly, just as Frankie did whenever Mom asked her that very same question. "I'll be home late. Around ten. Just so's you don't worry or anything. You still going to the movies with Annie?"

"Yeah—no—I don't know." *Annie*. Mom would persist in using that name as though her friend were still three years old. "Ann-*a* hasn't called."

"Well, if you do go, make sure Mrs. Green drives you

home afterward. You're sure you'll be okay?'' Mom's voice was normal, suddenly. Low, a little hoarse, and chronically anxious.

Frankie didn't reply.

''Francesca? I said, will you be okay?'' Mom's anxiety was hitting the red zone.

''Sure. I'm a brown belt, remember?'' Frankie retorted, then bit her tongue. Mom was making ominous noises about the karate class lately. About Frankie getting to be too much of a lady to punch it out with guys. Frankie hurriedly said good-bye and hung up, feeling strangely rattled. Mom, phoning like that, sounding all chatty, as if they were friends—at least, she'd sounded that way in the beginning. And her voice . . . It was getting so Frankie couldn't read her mother's moods any more. Like the times when Mom had just called Cape Canaveral to ask Dad for belated funds. Or was giving tests, and was stacked with papers to grade. Or was on the warpath. ''You're fifteen, now, Frankie, you should be wearing more feminine clothes.'' Frankie, who knew all the angles, couldn't figure this one.

She switched on the TV, cruised the channels for news of the fireball. Nothing, just the usual prehistoric cops and robbers and sentimental slush, and the news stations all at the sports stage. She came full circle, was just about to switch off, when a public service bulletin began to glide across the bottom of the screen.

Fireball hit lower Manhattan at five forty-eight P.M. *Outage stalled elevators and trains. Power quickly restored. No injuries reported. Meteorologists say freak lightning bolt caused by rapid changes in barometric pressure over the tri-state area . . . Repeat, fireball hit . . .*

Twice more the message passed across the screen. Frankie watched it, mesmerized. Then she zipped through the other channels. Business as usual.

Frankie snapped back to the original station, left it on. Lightning bolt? How about a UFO . . .? She sighed, remembering the evenings she and Dad had spent out in the yard, watching out for one, figuring what the aliens would be like inside. The good old days, that were not coming back. Well, she was fifteen now anyway, she told herself. Time to move on. To think of more adult things. Like getting out of school and into some worthwhile work. Like joining NASA. Or Greenpeace. Or some news outfit: to write on rain forests and oil spills, crusade to keep the world from going down the tubes.

Frankie caught sight of herself in the mantel mirror. Some crusader! She looked more like an urchin, with short, straight hair framing her small, unmemorable face, brown eyes, and nothing nose. Never mind. She had the look of Joan of Arc, sort of, somebody once said, though she couldn't recall exactly who. She raised her fist to her reflection in salute.

"I shall ride the star lanes," she cried. "Sail the high seas; fight to save the parrots and the dolphins and the trees!"

In the silence, the phone shrilled.

Frankie snatched up the receiver. *"Hello!"*

"Frankie?"

It was Anna. "Hi, old buddy!"

"Frankie—you okay?"

''Of course,'' Frankie said. ''What makes you think I'm not?''

''You sound a bit . . . strong.''

''That's because I *am* strong!'' Frankie cried, collapsing onto the couch. ''What's up?''

''Your mom home yet?''

Frankie sobered instantly. ''Nope. As a matter of fact, she's going to be late.'' Frankie had half a mind to mention her mother's strange behavior, decided not. Anna loved mystery and drama: start something now and she might not let it drop. ''Are we still going to the movies?''

''Why, sure. Pick you up in half an hour?''

''Okay—say,'' Frankie said quickly, before Anna could hang up. ''Did you hear about the fireball?''

''Fireball?''

''Never mind,'' Frankie said, and slowly replaced the receiver. Her breathing had subsided, and her excitement. She felt deflated now; and a little neglected. Why was Mom coming home late?

Frankie frowned slightly. Come to think, Mom was dressing up on Fridays. She'd even been to the beauty parlor and gotten a different hair cut . . . Frankie leapt to her feet. Half an hour, Anna had said. She ran into the kitchen and shoved the slice of frozen pizza into the microwave.

When Frankie got home from the movies, her mother was at the door, face flushed, eyes unusually bright. Frankie felt a prick of interest.

''Frankie,'' her mother said, turned her head to glance at herself in the hall glass. ''You doing anything tomorrow?''

"N n n-o."

"Good. I've a treat for you."

"Oh?"

"I thought we'd go into the city."

"Oh."

"There's a Whole Earth Show opening at the Natural History Museum."

"There is?" Frankie hadn't noticed that in the paper.

"Then after, we'll go on up to the Museum of the American Indian."

Two shows in one day! Frankie frowned suspiciously. "You serious?"

"I am."

"Okay," Frankie said, guardedly. She couldn't see how, but there had to be a catch there somewhere.

Her mother grabbed her and hugged her hard.

Frankie climbed thoughtfully between the sheets. Something was definitely up. There was a price tag somewhere, a biggie. *Two shows in one day. . . .* A price tag, an angle. With Mom, there always was. But she'd certainly go. She didn't know about the American Indian museum, she'd never been there, wasn't sure what there was to see, but the other? A Whole Earth Show!

Frankie had found the ad in the paper. Had read about the exhibits listed, from early fossils to moon rocks. Loads of stuff on the ecology, and whole rooms given over to space: the solar system, rockets, and interplanetary exploration. She lay back, her mind on sailing deep seas and deep space, until, coming full circle, she wondered again why Mom had come home late. She'd forgotten to ask. And Mom had neglected to say.

She thought of her father, and, wondering what he was doing just then, she leaned out, pulled a pack of well-worn snapshots from her nightstand drawer. She sifted through them, until she came to the one of Dad and his girlfriend Edie standing by their condominium pool: Dad in swimming shorts, Edie in a bright red bikini, both of them squinting up at the sun.

Two years, since Mom and Dad split up. For a while, she'd prayed it would all blow over, that Dad would come back home. Then Dad had met Edie. What a shock that had been. But Frankie had gotten over it, just about. And Edie seemed nice, even if she did always dress like she lived in a soap. Dad was happy, anyway.

Frankie sighed.

She should be grown up enough to feel cool. The old days when she was a kid wouldn't come back ever, anyhow. She turned the photos over: pictures of her and Dad playing basketball, football. Horsing around practicing karate moves. Swimming at Long Beach. Driving the hot rod he'd built her out of old mower parts. Her spaceship, they'd called it. The USS Enterprise Mark II. He'd promised to fit it with an electronic brain. But then there'd come the breakup, so he'd never gotten around to it. Pity. Dad was a genius. If he hadn't quit the Avery Aviation for Cape Canaveral, he'd be head of the whole computer department by now!

Why had he and Mom split up? It hadn't left Mom any happier. In fact, she'd gotten grim, somehow, and . . . stiff. Not like Aunt Maggie. Frankie turned to a photo of Mom's younger sister—at least, as much as you could see past Cricket and Jocko: black Dobermans, leaping shoulder-high—stealing the camera as usual. Frankie had been on the farm west-northwest of Montreal in Canada only the summer before. She remembered standing in their very back yard with the old gray barn and the big red door, and the misty Laurentian foothills behind, right beside Uncle Jim while he snapped that very shot. Frankie loved going up there. The air was clean and the land beautiful. And life seemed so much easier up there, and the problems, far away. She put the snapshots back and shut the drawer. With luck she and Mom would go there again this year, as soon as school was over.

Frankie put out the light, curled up on her side, and turned once more to wondering what was on her mother's mind. Whatever it was, it was big. And, of this Frankie was certain, whatever it was, she was just about to find it out. . . .

SKY-FIRE-TRAIL

It was cold and dark. The people huddled close over their small fires. Outside the hide shelters, the angry wind spirits snarled fitfully, sweeping the bare trees, bending the reeds over the nearby marsh. Not a soul was about, not out on the snowy ground between the tents, not by the enormous oak where the trail entered the village. Nothing, no one broke upon the cold emptiness of that spring night, until, all at once from overhead came a loud thundercrack. A moment later, a blast of air burst against the hide shelters, shaking fish-drying poles down from their frames. The first explosion over, the wind remained; a fierce, long, even current, a giant's breath to blow the village away.

A head poked out from one tipi, then another and another. Soon folk were emerging from every tent—save one whose flap remained shut. They gathered among the tipis, murmuring, looking about. Someone shouted, pointing to a speck, a spark of brilliant light high above.

While they watched, the light cut an arc toward them, growing in size and intensity, giving off a trail of brilliant flame.

The crowd shrank in together; silent, awed.

Nearer it came, and nearer, coming straight at them. The people began to shuffle backward, muttering uncertainly, still staring up. One man, head and shoulders above the rest, called out harshly, shook a tall, fur-trimmed hickory spear at them, urging them to stand their ground and watch.

But at a loud boom as from one hundred thunderclaps, the people dropped to the ground, the tall man with them. Another blast bent the tree tops, plucked one tipi from its moorings and blew it away along the frozen ground. The people pressed themselves into the earth.

The fireball passed over the tent tops, vanished behind the ridge bordering the marsh. The ground shook, and the prostrate villagers covered their heads as the night air filled with a hissing and spitting as from a thousand angry wildcats. A moment later, there arose above the treetops a great, glowing cloud of sulfurous steam.

The wind died, the tree became still. But the glowing steam remained. One by one in the quiet, the villagers raised their heads, slowly climbed to their feet, and stood uncertainly.

Then the tall man led the villagers to the edge of the settlement, to gaze at the strange glowing cloud rising from the swamp. The man spoke, pointed his hickory spear first toward it, then at the tent from which still no one emerged. Just then, there came from that tipi a loud and urgent sound, followed by a second, not as loud, maybe, yet more commanding in its urgency: a hoarse and vital human noise—a newborn child's first cry.

"The radio, Francesca!" Frankie's mother yelled. "Turn it off, right now! I can't hear myself think!"

Frankie reduced it slowly and reluctantly to the level of the noise in the car.

"Off! Right off—or you'll only turn it up again!"

Tight-lipped, Frankie cut the song, one of her favorites, and almost through. Agh, best to let it go. They'd already had one fight and it wasn't even nine o'clock. She hunkered down resignedly in her seat, staring up at the sagging skies, half-wishing she'd not agreed to go; that she'd arranged a later visit to the exhibition with Anna instead.

"Don't sprawl. You'll crease up your pants."

Frankie shifted, came up, then slid down again, squinting along the length of her blue wool-clad legs to her brown suede loafers. Who in the world was better than Mom at spoiling what promised to be a neat day? Could somebody explain how all this preppy stuff was better than jeans and hightops?

And it could have been worse. Mom had tried to back her

into a tweed skirt and high-heeled boots like her own; the stuff that she'd insisted on buying for Frankie on their last mall trip together. A total waste, Frankie would see to that. You can lead a horse to water, she thought, mutinously, but you can't make it drink!

It had, however, taken courage that morning to force the compromise. Frankie glanced sideways. Mom was nervous. Uptight. About what? She turned back to the windshield, feeling a twinge of the previous night's uneasiness. She remembered her horoscope. "Significant event today will change your life . . ." Agh, silly things, horoscopes. Good for a laugh. Still. Strange how since last night she had this funny feeling that something was about to break. . . .

The Whole Earth Show was even better than Frankie had expected. There were mock-ups of Earth first forming, and cooling. One display, suggesting that Earth's atmosphere had once been anaerobic, showed the development of creatures to whom oxygen was a poison. Frankie bent closer to read how Earth had "hiccupped" at one point, tipping the balance to an oxygen-bearing biosphere. It seemed that at that point, the anaerobic life had become all but extinct, poisoned by the oxygen. Now, only a few minute species remained; bacteria groups confined to places such as bogs and lake floors.

Depicting this change were drawings and diagrams and models of Earth seen as a single living being called Gaia, with heart and lungs and so on. The primal forests were the lungs, drawing in the carbon dioxide and nitrogen wastes and giving off oxygen by photosynthesis. Beautiful, Frankie thought, to think of the world as one live entity, like a person—a woman, with that name! Frankie pictured Gaia: beautiful, healthy, glowing with life—until they came to the next exhibit. This warned of an ailing ecosystem: all was not well with Gaia. She was sick, and could get sicker. There was talk of the greenhouse effect, of mine and forest stripping, of poison in the seas and the atmosphere. There were photographs of deserts where once bush and forest had flourished; acres of dead and bloated fish clogging polluted lakes and waterways. The all-too-familiar shots of piled-up dead birds and seals on the Alaskan shores. Frankie moved on quickly to pictures of efforts to put things right: of reforestation, of massive rescue efforts to save endangered species from extinction. Of the efforts of such outfits as Greenpeace, and the World Wildlife Fund, and the voluntary Student Conservation Association: hundreds and thousands of people striving to save the environment and animal species from extinction.

Not enough. Frankie looked around with misgiving. The scale of the problems was immense compared with the effort to solve them. She thought back to the previous night, how she had posed in front of the glass, her fist raised in resolution. *I shall ride the star lanes, sail the high seas; fight to save the parrots and the dolphins and the trees . . .* The mighty crusader! What could one person do in the face of such overwhelming devastation?

Mom's arm slipped around her shoulders. "Tough, isn't it, hon? We want progress, but where do you draw the line?"

Soberly, they moved on.

The next exhibits depicted life evolving in the new ecosystem, beginning with simple-celled amoeba and culminating in its highest form: mankind. Not that the process was finished, so the blurb said. The human mind even now was on the threshold of unprecedented breakthroughs, both in the design of artificial intelligence and new techniques in cloning and DNA engineering. Fascinated, Frankie read how, in the not-too-distant future, "there will be walking undetected among us artificial human clones and androids, as well as hybrid cyborgs."

"Ugh." Frankie's mother nudged her on. "O Brave New World! I sure hope I'm not here to see them!"

Frankie couldn't resist. "I'll bet that's what Australopithecus said about Homo erectus. *I* think it's exciting."

The next exhibit was a mock-up of a city one hundred years ahead: streamlined, clean, futuristic aerial walkways threading tall towers, gleaming capsules zooming through the air, silver monorails and moving pavements crowded with mylar-suited pedestrians.

Her mother tugged at her arm. "Come on, Frankie. There's still so much more to see. We'll never get around it all at this rate."

Frankie hung back. "Just a sec." She leaned down, peering closely in among the towers, picturing herself going up in one of those mach-speed elevators to the umpteenth floor to gaze out over the shining metropolis. . . .

"I can't understand you, Frankie," her mother said impatiently. "One minute you're sickening over the state of the environment, and the next you're gung ho over all this!" Mom waved her arm about in disgust.

"So? Past and future needn't be at odds."

"Oh no? Frankie, even now you complain how there's hardly any green in this place outside of Central Park! Well look there." She pointed to the new and shining city. "There's not a single leaf or blade anywhere."

True, Frankie had to admit. And she'd been too carried away by the novelty of it all to notice. It certainly was an oversight by the showcase designers. Maybe she could write and let them know, she thought, moving on.

In the space section, there were not only rockets and moon rocks, but photographs, drawings, laser projections; scale models of Mars and Venus and all the other planets; computer-generated dioramas of their landscapes.

Mom, patently uninterested in Dad's field, moved on, toward the exit. But Frankie dawdled past every display, pausing at the pictures of NASA launches, peering into lighted display panels, at shots of the launch control room with the operators at their terminals. Frankie searched their faces, even though these pictures had been taken before Dad's time.

At the astronaut exhibit, Frankie scanned photographs and drawings of projected manned landing sites on the moon and Mars and Venus; and shuttles descending, picturing herself in one of them, feeling—how?—minutes from stepping out onto alien ground. She pressed for filmstrips of the crews in training: in free fall, before mock-up controls, rehearsing their launch routines. Six women. Frankie's eyes gleamed. She might be there one day, in that training program. . . .

"Frankie!" Mom was walking purposefully toward her.

"Coming," she said, and pulled herself away. Together, they made for the exit.

On the way back to the car, Mom steered Frankie into a coffee shop. Puzzled, Frankie followed her inside. Mom wasn't one to snack.

Frankie ordered a vanilla shake; Mom, coffee, black, as usual.

"Well," Mom said brightly. "That was really interesting. I certainly hope the American Indian museum proves as good."

"Umph," Frankie said. And wondered why they hadn't simply gone straight there. Her mother stirred her coffee rapidly, swilling it over onto her saucer, then frowning, tugged a paper napkin out of the table dispenser and mopped up the overflow.

"When we get there," her mother went on, inspecting her coffee minutely, "there's . . . someone I want you to meet."

Frankie sighed in release. Was that all? While Frankie granted she might not have been exactly gracious to certain of Mom's friends in the past, two trips in one day was a generous bribe. . . . "That's okay. She having lunch with us?"

Her mother bit her lip. "Frankie—it's a him."

"Him?"

Her mother began to talk, in a rush. "My professor at Hunter, Dr. Webb. He wants to meet you." Mom's face was bright red now.

Frankie watched the color deepening, fascinated. "Why?"

"He's interested in you."

"Why?"

"Oh, Francesca! I've told him all about you."

"Why?" Frankie's gaze sharpened. "Is he—after you?"

Her mother looked down. Heavens, she said, whatever gave Frankie that idea. Bingham was a good teacher, and conscientious, helping her such a lot—as he was helping everyone else, Mom added quickly. She was getting so much out of the course, she was grateful. The least she—and Frankie—could do was to accept Dr. Webb's invitation gracefully. So like it or not, her mother's voice rose, she and Frankie would go to meet him, now, at the American Indian museum, then eat a meal with him.

So that was why the detour. First the bribe, then the setup—then the payoff. Mom had set her up, and was now paving the way, so's Frankie would be nice to this Webb guy, and not be awkward. After all, she had been a daddy's girl . . . Frankie tried to picture herself walking with this strange man, sitting across from him at a public table.

"Well, Frankie? What do you say?"

Frankie shrugged. "Okay." What choice did she have?

Mom stood up. "Please be nice," she said, a wheedle in her voice.

"I said okay," Frankie retorted, caught the hurt in her mother's face.

As they pulled from the curb, Frankie gazed out at the pedestrians bent into the bitter wind, holding onto hats, scarves, upturned collars. Scraps of paper soared like dirty gulls, fell back to lie with empty food cartons, styrofoam cups, and soda cans. Pigeons fought and foraged in the gutter. Peck, peck, peck.

It was a long—and thoughtful—drive, up Broadway to 155th, under the subway trestle that spanned the Harlem dip, and up the slowly mounting street count. Sunlight cut the windshield; cheap, bright spangle-gold; blinding. Frankie pulled down her visor.

"You're very quiet, Frankie," Mom said at last.

"Uh-huh." Frankie looked down at her worsted knees. She had a funny feeling in the pit of her stomach. She was being a brat, and knew it, and wanted to snap out of it somehow. When we get there, she promised herself, I'll come right, I'll show Mom I can behave. But, oh, one thought kept running through her head. Whatever she said, and he said, and however nice the guy might be, *he wasn't Dad.*

Bingham Webb was waiting by the door.

Frankie hung back, let her mother get there first. He was tall, long, stoopy. Pale straight hair, slicked back. Gold-rimmed glasses. Frankie noted the crumpled raincoat, the scuffed suede boots. Dark plaid collar, knitted green tie. Hardly Mom's type, she thought. Dad was stocky, straight, and, like Frankie, not exactly tall. In high heels beside Dad, Mom came out ahead—though you always noticed Dad. Frankie's throat caught. She felt like a traitor, standing there. She wanted to turn right around, walk away.

Her mother, barely coming to Webb's shoulder, looked up as he stepped out to greet them. "Dr. Webb, my daughter

Francesca—Frankie. Frankie, my professor, Dr. Bingham Webb."

"Hi, Frankie." Webb reached out, Frankie stuck her hand in his and looked him straight in the eye. "Hi, Dr. Webb."

"Oh, call me Bingham, please." He smiled down at her, and to her surprise, she found herself almost smiling back, despite the direness of it all. He turned to her mother. "You really want to take the tour right now, Celia? This girl has hungry eyes."

Celia, thought Frankie.

"We do," Mom said. "Absolutely. Lunch can wait."

Bingham Webb ushered them inside.

Frankie followed, watching. Webb took her mother's hand; after a moment, Mom retrieved it, with a quick glance at Frankie. Frankie looked the other way. They moved into the first gallery, Frankie's attention divided between her mother and Webb, and the surrounding displays.

At the third showcase, Frankie pulled up. Peering down at bits of carved shell: white *wampum* made from tubular periwinkle, purple *sewan* made from quahog, she read how those bits were adopted as currency by Dutch settlers short of regular cash. Neat. And those shells lay around local beaches this very day, ignored.

They moved past carved pipes, and brittle medicine cases decorated with feathers and sacred tokens all with special meanings, Webb said. Frankie studied the carvings, and the cards telling what each thing was, trying to picture them all bright and new.

Upstairs was a large showcase displaying a model of a Delaware Indian village that, supposedly, had existed on Manhattan upward of a thousand years ago. ''Doesn't look Indian,'' she murmured. The tipis were not fancy tipis like you saw in the movies, but rough shelters made from animal hide stretched over simple frames. The villagers were not done up in feathers and fancy beaded leggings, but wore only plain pelts and furs. Of course. Bingham Webb had already explained how the glass beads had come with the white man. Before that, the Indians had decorated their things, and much better, too, Frankie thought, with natural wampum and sewan, and quills. To one side of the tiny clustered shelters, drying fish hung on poles. Women washed clothes by the painted river's edge, and naked children played at their feet.

Frankie shivered, thinking of the bright and shining future city in the Whole Earth Show. People in that place would never have to suffer the natural elements, whatever the season. This little settlement was so primitive, those hide shelters looked so flimsy and exposed. And those trees . . . bare. It was obviously winter. ''How come those people don't freeze to death?'' Frankie murmured.

''They were hardened to the cold,'' Webb explained. ''This is how the local Delaware tribes—Manhattan, Canarsie—lived before the white man came. We call this period *the Precontact Era.*''

She watched his mouth forming the words. A friendly mouth. Kind. She'd watched it over the last hour, observed it curving up into a well-worn smile. Frankie turned back to the model. Dusty and dark, the very sight of it made her want to sneeze. "Those kids aren't wearing any clothes at all."

"That's because they're not yet of age. Boys run naked until they're through the rites of huskanaw."

Frankie looked up. "Husky, what?"

Webb's eyes gleamed behind their frames. "Huskanaw. Like bar mitzvah, kind of. Actually, it's not a Delaware term, but it serves. The boys go through trials to prove their manhood. Some of them, quite dangerous, lasting through ten, twenty days. But it was a tough life; they had to prove their endurance; learn to survive."

"And the girls?"

"Well, it was so long ago, who's to say for sure? Some scholars argue that the women shared these tasks, to an extent differing from tribe to tribe. In that case, they'd have taken the rites too, I guess."

"What do you think?"

Webb shook his head. "I believe that here the men were the hunters and the fishers, the ones to take the risks."

Mom spoke up. "Oh? I suppose having children didn't count."

Webb blinked, momentarily put out. "Celia, you're right. The death rate of mothers and children was pretty high. So I suppose they went through their own huskanaw."

"And no second chances," Mom said.

"Touché." Webb grinned. "I think I'd better watch my tongue!"

And how, Frankie thought. She was still piqued over the boys-only huskanaw. "Girls always miss the fun."

''Francesca!''

''Hardly fun, Frankie,'' Webb said. ''Be glad you missed it.''

''Missed, like, what?''

Webb considered. ''Well, you might have had to go out into the forest alone to bag a deer. Or perform some feat in water.''

''Swim a race?'' Frankie swam well.

''Not exactly. Apologies to Longfellow, but they didn't go for our kind of competition—you know: seeing who is fastest or strongest.''

''What then?'' What other kind of competition was there?

''You'd maybe have to reenact some tribal myth, like, let's see. . . .'' Webb looked up to the ceiling. ''Dive to the bottom of the Hudson.''

Frankie shuddered, thinking of the bitter spring cold outside. ''What for?''

''To reenact the world's creation. You see those people held that, in the beginning, the muskrat dove to the ocean floor and came up with a scoop of mud, and placed it on the turtle's back.''

''And so?''

''And so you might be made to fetch a fistful of mud from the riverbed, repeating the performance.''

Frankie nodded, thinking. The Hudson was deep; the current, deadly. You'd die fast right now from hypothermia. But she was a good swimmer and diver—on the school team this year. And didn't Mr. Ho always say that she was one tough cookie? She pictured herself standing on one of those rocks overlooking the river's edge. *Naked?* Well, maybe with her navy suit on. She set her feet, took a deep breath, and dove.

It would be light at first, of course. But as she went deeper it would grow darker, and very cold. She'd have to kick hard. It was difficult to stay deep under water, especially with a lungful of air, she knew that from experience. She imagined letting a trail of bubbles up toward the light. Then, reaching the bottom, she'd scrabble through soft slime on the river bed until she hit mud. There! Frankie's fist tightened unconsciously. Her hand would close about it, and with a quick kick of her legs, she'd then shoot back up to the surface, and with her powerful front crawl, cut in to the bank.

She imagined the Elders, marveling, leaning down to help her out.

''You did great, kiddo,'' they'd say, or words to that effect.

Frankie, coughing a little, opened her hand, displaying the lump of rich black mud with pride. ''No big deal,'' she said aloud. ''Now what?''

Bingham Webb eyed her over the rim of his glasses. ''Well, the Elders might haze you, flog you some—''

Frankie was indignant. ''*Flog* me?'' After all that?

''To prove your will and endurance. Or they might shut you up alone, for hours, maybe days.''

''What *for?*''

''To induce an altered mental state by what we call today 'sensory deprivation.' They'd stick you someplace dark and quiet away from outside stimuli—company, noise, food, and such—until you had some kind of vision.''

Frankie frowned. ''What if I didn't?'' She could just imagine Mom parked outside, waiting for results.

''No problem. They'd give you a mild psychedelic herb to help you along. You'd have your vision, describe it, and the Elders would decide what your adult role was to be—if they hadn't already guessed.''

''How?''

''Say a spear figured in your vision: you'd likely be a hunter, or a warrior, depending on what else you saw.''

''What if I wanted to be something else?''

Webb shrugged. ''You wouldn't. You dreamed: you became.''

Oh, really? Frankie shrugged also. If she didn't want to become whatever, she'd simply make up some other dream to suit herself! She gazed at the rugged, dusty landscape, put herself in one of those holes among the rocks: cold, hungry, waiting in the dark for some kind of sign. Ugh. Compared with that, vocational guidance was a breeze.

Behind the model was an aerial shot of the same landscape, present day. Some woodland left, but most was now built-up; brownstone apartments, shops, and traffic-choked streets. ''Whatever happened to those people, and their settlement?'' she muttered, thinking back to the Whole Earth Show.

''They were assimilated, Frankie. There as everywhere else.''

Assimilated? Sounded sinister: threatening. Like *annihilated.*

''Well, Frankie?'' Mom said, prodding her to make some comment. Bingham Webb was obviously awaiting a response. Something popped in Frankie. She couldn't think why; maybe she was tired. Two shows in one go was a bit much, even if you liked that kind of thing. And a whole morning of Mom on top of that? Now here her mother was, waiting for her to *perform*. Frankie looked down at the village, the magic gone. It was just a motley jumble of painted plaster, dried twigs, and lumps of mud-covered styrofoam. A made-up thing, by people who claimed to know so much about a past so distant that who was going to challenge them?

"How do you know all this?" she demanded suspiciously. "Prove it!"

"Francesca!"

Frankie glared back. "He wasn't there," she said. "Nobody was."

"*Francesca!*" Mom said, really loud this time, then looked around, embarrassed, as people stared.

But Bingham Webb seemed pleased. "Good point, Frankie. You'd make an excellent history scholar. In fact, we'll get back to it later. Right now—" He took both their elbows and steered them firmly toward the stairs. "I, for one, am starving. Let's go *eat!*"

Hahn came to lying on the floor. He kept quite still, just as he was, on his back, and checked his damage systematically. Skeletal structure: minor torque, eighth vertebra; slight disturbance, rear cranium; more severe contusion behind his left ear. But all easily fixed, though it would take time. He wrinkled his nose. Rotten smell, fog in the cabin. Olfactory scanners still working, then. He raised his head, and wished he hadn't. His inner gyroscopes were off, he learned, as the cabin walls slowly revolved around him; field scanners a little shaky, too, blurring his vision. So much for him.

Had he managed to land without hurting anyone?

Hahn glanced around. The holoboxes were dead. And much of the instrumentation. Though not— In dismay, Hahn contemplated a large, red crystal, larger and lighter in color than the somber doomsday stone—his *interact* alarm. Like the doomsday button, it was fail-safe: even if the ship were totally destroyed, it would, like the other, perform its functions still. Right now, it was blinking, like a slow beacon, on and off, filling him with misgiving. Somehow, it warned, the crash had affected this planet's space/time continuum, had interacted somehow with its history—though at the moment of impact, the effect had been only small. But negligible as it was, if left uncorrected, odds were the change his crash had caused would grow and grow, resulting in who knows what disaster?

Hahn clapped his hands to his head. He was damaged, the ship was damaged, a former ally hunted him down—and on top of all that he'd broken one of ISPYC's cardinal rules!

To what extent?

One thing at a time, Hahn told himself. Before he could determine that, he must put himself and the ship to rights—as far as that was possible. He pulled himself up with effort, and, leaning against the wall, stuck a finger into a data port, taking his bearings, scanning for damage.

He appeared to have landed close by the place where he'd seen the signs Broad and Wall streets. They were gone, of course, left behind in the future. How far back had the ship fled before the time controls had stalled? One thousand, four hundred and fifty-one Earth years, the answer came instantly. Not long. Certainly not long enough to be safe from the other H.A.H.N.'s pursuit.

For what length of time had he lain unconscious on the cabin floor? For upward of twelve Earth hours, Hahn's own built-in (and seemingly intact) chronometer said.

And the ship? The damage was extensive. Apart from the instrumentation, both ship's drives—stellar and local propulsion—were dead. Right now, Hahn's craft couldn't budge one Earth millimeter, not if his life depended on it.

Were they smashed beyond repair? He wouldn't know until the ship had run its restoration cycle. There was also the hole in the hull.

Hahn lurched over to the gaping breach and ran his fingertips around the jagged edge. Bad enough, though another few degrees and a main terminal would have been demolished also. Hahn put his face to the hole and peered through. Felt oddly disturbing, for the ship's interior, which had been up to this point like an hermetically sealed eggshell, to be cracked open onto this alien world; for him to be drawing its air directly into his lungs: a raw atmosphere, ripe with the fleshy smell of rotted vegetation and stinking gases. It was daylight out there now—diffused by thick fog, probably from the ship's exhausts. He remembered the swamp he'd glimpsed, just before the crash. Rough shelters, tents, nearby.

Hahn felt a stab of worry, reassured himself that he couldn't have actually injured anyone, or the interact alarm would be going at a rate. But whatever ill he'd started out there, he reminded himself, he couldn't amend it while he and the ship were in their present state. Both needed time for repairs. He turned back to the monitor wall, a little too quickly, setting the cabin a-spin around him. Standard procedure in this kind of emergency required him to dematerialize the ship to avoid the slightest chance of contact with native inhabitants. Was the random-oscillator still working? Hahn pressed for dematerialization, and breathed out in relief as the controls responded. Not that anything appeared to happen inside the cabin. But through the hole in the cabin wall, the outside world vanished to a grayish blur, just as, to anyone watching from out there, the ship also would have faded and disappeared, like smoke, leaving an empty dip in the marsh mud which rapidly filled with water.

But although Hahn had dematerialized, removing the ship from that world's space/time continuum, he was still a sitting target for his old ally-turned-enemy.

What to do?

Perhaps, Hahn reasoned, he ought to get moving again. Moving targets were much more difficult to pin down. But how to do that, with the ship's drives dead? Hahn weighed his options. If he couldn't shift through space, perhaps he should do as before and move through time alone—*if* the time controls still worked.

Hahn touched the white quartz time button, tapped for start, and nodded with satisfaction at the prompt response. Only stalled, as he had hoped. Should he, Hahn wondered, edge the ship forward by degrees at a slow, uniform rate, reversing the time-travel flow back toward the moment of entry into Earth's atmosphere? Risky. Once the process was engaged, the ship would have to stay in random-oscillation mode, lest it materialize inside something solid that would occupy the same point in the space/time continuum somewhen in the future. There were safeguards, of course, to prevent such a disaster, but Hahn had no idea if they were working or not.

There was another risk in using the time stone: when in operation, it emitted a distinctive signal which the enemy could detect. What if he did? *And while Hahn was defenseless in the LSRM?*

Another risk, but one that Hahn must take.

He tapped the order in, then set the time controls on automatic, eyeing the interact alarm thoughtfully. Even at this rate, the temporal difference between inside and outside the ship could grow quite marked. Because although inside the cabin, repairs should take just *hours,* time outside the ship would be shifting at the rate of *years.* . . . What if the effect of his crash upon those people became critical while he was still in the LSRM? Hahn weighed the odds, stayed with his choice.

Now he looked to the ship's repairs. His head whirling, he struggled to correct the ship's stabilizers, set its energy banks on recharge, then ordered up a scan of all other systems and linked them to automatic repair. Swiftly, his hands moved about the walls, tapping out the correct codes for the damaged instrumentation. Then, at a touch on an orange crystal, a nozzle snaked out of the silver cabin roof, writhed slowly by his head, waiting. Another short, sharp, rhythmic sequence, and the nozzle sought the breach in the wall, then, whirring softly, began to exude metal alloy, around and around the edge of the scar until eventually it would close the hole up, then harden. Two hours, and the ship's shell would be good as new.

Hahn's sight was blurring worse than ever now; his gyroscopes were failing, and, with them, his balance. He fell dizzily against the wall. He'd done all he had to: from this point the ship would mend itself, as far as it was able. Now to fix his own needs—and only just in time!

Hahn summoned the LSRM up out of the floor, almost smiling to see it. He shouldn't feel anything, of course, for he wasn't programmed to think of his own comfort, but the sight of that silver case emerging, like a giant cocoon, gave him such a sense of safety.

He tapped out the correct repair combination, set the outside controls on automatic, raised the padded lid, and fell in. He stretched out full length, placed the silver cap on his head, and was just relaxing when he became aware of a slight, unpleasant sensation in his cranium, just behind his left ear. Strange. Hahn frowned up at the cabin ceiling. What it was he knew full well, by name. But *experience* it? He winced slightly as the unpleasantness increased. How, or why, this was happening to him, Hahn could not imagine. Yet, unaccountably, he felt pleased. "So this is what humans suffer when they're injured," he said to himself, then he whispered the name those humans knew it by up in those teeming, crowded streets: "Pain."

He reached for means to block it, let his hand fall back to his side, as, with a *whuff* of air, the LSRM lid clamped shut, blocking outer sound. In the padded silence of that closed space, instruments slid quietly from their ports in the cylinder's sides, began their healing work. Hahn slowed down his entire metabolism and closed his eyes. The pain was easing already, just as it would in a real human being. He was repairing fast; and his ship also. A few more Earth hours, cabin time—years, to the folk out there—and ship and scout would both be good as new.

. . .

The Elders stood on the edge of the swamp, the boy beside them. The leader, Chief Tallspear, the boy's uncle, foster father, turned to the man at his elbow. ''Well, Dreamwalker? Are the omens right? Does he meet the great swamp spirit now?''

Dreamwalker grunted from the folds of his cloak, gazed out over the watery waste in the failing light. Then shook his head. ''No. Not yet.''

Tallspear's brows came down. ''Tomorrow, the boy counts twelve turns of the sun. We cannot delay any longer his time of huskanaw.''

Dreamwalker nodded. ''Therefore at the next turn of the sun, on the eve of his twelfth birthday, he comes as a man. Perhaps this is as it is meant to be. Perhaps this is what the great swamp spirit awaits. In any case, I tell you, the omens are not yet right.''

At these words, Tallspear led the group back toward the settlement.

The boy followed, eyeing the backs of the men ahead. Excitement stirred within him. Every year, for as long as he could remember, it had been the same. On the eve of each successive birthday, the walk to the swamp, the wait while Dreamwalker read the signs.

Then Tallspear's question: Is it time? Dreamwalker's reply: Not yet. The walk back. The times when he'd plucked up courage to ask what it was about, Dreamwalker wouldn't say. Perhaps, the boy thought irreverently, it was because Dreamwalker didn't know. All they'd tell him was that one day when they made that journey, the men would go back without him. He'd hoped that it would be this year—as part of his time of huskanaw. Tomorrow marked the beginning of his thirteenth year, when he would become a man. But Dreamwalker had said the omens were not yet right: that he must wait another year. The boy quickened his stride, almost treading on an Elder's heels. Tomorrow, he'd be a man at last. Nothing would take that from him.

The next day was bright and cold. In a high, white sky, the sun flashed off the Shatemuc, the icy Mahicanituk. From their perch on the Place of Hanging Rocks, the Elders leaned over, looking down into the swirling tide.

Chief Tallspear beckoned the boy forward.

"It is time, son of my beloved sister, Shining Leaf. As the great muskrat dove deep for earth to place on the turtle's back and create the world, so I say that you must now become as he, braving the Mahicanituk to bring us back like token."

With his spear, the chief signaled the naked boy to dive.

The boy looked down at the shining ripples. Only hours before, the current had been capped with rigid ice, and this night it would be so again. His flesh cringed at the thought of cutting that cold surface.

"We wait." Tallspear urged him forward.

Rising to his toes, the boy dove in.

All at once, he felt the water's claim upon his body. He fought against the forceful swirl that pulled him to the deadly sharp rock place: *kau-p-si*. Kicking hard, he went down, and the deeper he went, the more his head hurt. Down, down, he went, into a darker region, where the water pressed in upon him like giant hands, and the current roared in his ears. The pain in his head sharpened, and lights flashed behind his eyes. But he set his mind grimly to endure. If he was to succeed, he must not waver, not forget that he was He Who Trails In Fire Across The Starry Heavens, and that he must bring up from the river floor a measure of mud even as the great muskrat once had done in the beginning of the world.

The pain passed. Now large, gray shadows brushed by him in the darkness. Surely he had drifted into the domain of the water spirits. Was he dreaming, or awake? Ghostly faces floated before him, pale in the darkness; stern, sad men with dark eyes fixed upon him.

His conscious thought flowed out with the streaming, formless tide, until he lost his name, and all knowledge of his waking identity. No longer was he boy, diving as once muskrat had done; he *was* muskrat reincarnate: the very one on whom the whole wide world depended, who must go to the bottom of all things and bring up one small, solid truth on which to stay the people. . . .

His kicks grew feeble; his legs, numb. New currents more powerful by far from those above sought to pull him two ways: upward back to the surface, and in the direction of their flow. But even in his exalted state, some part of him remained aware of his urgent danger, a river with form and power enough to sweep the strongest swimmer downstream and hurl him upon the Place of Sharp Rocks. He thrust his lean brown body down farther, fighting to keep his strength, not for himself, but for the clan. If he went out on the current, so would they. Down he went, deeper, reaching for the riverbed.

Just as he was beginning to despair, his groping hands scraped stone, and below that, encountered silty mud. This, this was what he had come for, a new world to set beneath the people's feet. He scooped up a handful, and, fired by success, flexed his knees, pushed his feet against the slimy floor, and propelled himself back with his prize.

Mud streamed through his fingers, even as he rose up through the waters. By the time he reached the Elders, it would be gone, and he'd have risked all for nothing! He tightened his frozen fingers as best he could, but still the mud streamed, so he cupped one hand over the other, and squeezed. Pain came back, suddenly. Cold split his head, his very bones ached through his numb, bloodless flesh. Without arms to propel him, his body began to twist and roll, making him afraid.

That fear brought him to his senses. He looked upward through the darkness. Where was the sunlight? Which way? Which way? Perhaps he'd dove too deep, perhaps he'd never find his way back into the everyday world. And he'd have failed his people. What would they say, his foster father, Chief Tallspear? His mother, Shining Leaf? And what would Dreamwalker say, when he did not reappear?

And what would become of his people?

His chest was close to bursting. Light flared like the sun across his inward vision. Air, he must have *air!* He forced his legs into one last kick—all he had strength for—then opened his mouth onto wild gray water. Waves surged about his shoulders as arms reached down and grabbed him.

They pulled him up retching and gasping for breath. Rocks ripped his legs and his blood ran down, splashing into the tide.

How far had the waters carried him from his starting place? He caught a glimpse of figures strung out along the bank, running swiftly toward him. He couldn't tell. No matter.

He remembered how, deep in the cold, dark regions of the water spirits, human boy had ceased to be; had merged with muskrat, knowing clearly, as the sun makes the day, that in his hands lay the survival of his people.

He tried to raise his head. Where was Tallspear? Dreamwalker? He must tell what he had become down there, the urgent truth he'd seen. He fell back again, exhausted. His face, his lips, his mind were frozen. He could not speak. Never mind . . . later.

As they lifted him from the water's edge, he raised hands he could no longer feel. He parted them, and held them out, and there, in his cupped and wrinkled palm, a tiny pat of green-black mud remained.

Sunday afternoon, Frankie went with Anna to the mall. All morning, she thought about what she would say to Anna, about the museum trip, and Bingham Webb. About how Mom had sprung this guy on her, how she'd been braced to dislike him, and how neat he was, after all, though quite different from Dad. About how great it was that Mom had gotten a boyfriend, and how it might take some heat off Frankie. However, as soon as they met, she found herself talking about everything but. Even when she faced Anna in Peaches and Cream, where they always got down to it, she hedged, batting around her hot fudge sundae, and babbling about the Whole Earth Show, and what the American Indian museum had been like. Not a word of Bingham Webb.

". . . and we didn't get home until five-thirty. I was wiped!" Frankie spooned up some cream and slapped it down again. "I mean, there was so much to see in both places. You'd need to go back a second time."

"Tell me . . ." Anna began.

''What?''

''What you liked the best.''

''Oh, goodness, that's impossible. There were super displays on the environment and the ecology—you know, the rain forests, and the—''

''Oh, please!'' Anna made a face. ''Spare the doom and gloom today. What about the fun stuff—like the robots and spaceships they listed in the ads?''

Frankie rolled her eyes. ''The robotics section was fab, you've no idea! It wasn't what you'd think—you know—metal claws and rivets. It was about . . .'' She screwed up her eyes in an effort to remember. '' 'Who knows, but in just a few years from now, there will be walking undetected among us artificial human clones and androids, as well as hybrid cyborgs.' ''

''Ugh.'' Anna shuddered. ''What's a cyborg?''

''Put it this way,'' Frankie said, knowing her friend's limitations. ''You know how a clone is an exact copy of another living being? And an android is your wholly mechanical robot? Well, a cyborg is a kind of hybrid; a mixture of the two.''

''You mean part man, part machine?'' Anna made a face.

''Hey, come on,'' Frankie said. ''What about old man Robinson down the road with a pacemaker? And that guy last month who got the artificial heart? And Chris Emerson: he lost his leg, and he's playing baseball. Not to mention all the other people you read about in the papers with artificial arms and legs—even voice boxes.''

''I suppose,'' Anna said, doubtfully.

''So where do you draw the line? Say someone gets all

smashed up in a car crash? I mean really smashed. Who's going to say how much he or she can have replaced with artificial parts and still be human?''

Anna was looking most uncomfortable now. ''Let's change the subject. What about the space section?''

Frankie told Anna about the space and astronaut exhibits, and the pictures of the NASA launch center. ''It was *so-o-o* neat. I called Dad last night about it and we talked for hours.'' Mostly about the robotics, actually, but better not get back onto that again. Her father had said that he was thinking of shifting into robotics himself. It was the wave of the future, he said, and he wanted to catch it. He'd offered to send Frankie a book on it; nothing too technical, just general stuff she'd understand. Of course, she'd said yes. Anything that interested Dad, interested Frankie too.

Anna leaned forward, put her elbows on the table. ''What was *he* like?''

''Who?''

''Frankie! You know perfectly well. *Him*. Dr. Webb.''

Webb? Frankie was dumbfounded. ''How—who told you?''

''Your mom told my mom about him, that's how. He sounds nice.''

Frankie sat, shocked. Anna knew about the man? Behind her back?

Misreading her, Anna jumped in deeper than ever. ''Hey, you look mad,'' she said. ''What's the matter, don't you want your mom to be happy, Frankie?''

''What's that to do with you?'' Frankie set down her spoon.

"Ooops, *sorry!*" Anna said, not sounding it one bit.

"Oh, don't be." Frankie's anger flared. "Since you know so much, why not just go on?"

"Okay." Anna bit her lip, then said in a rush, "Dr. Webb likes your mom a lot, you know? And your mom told my mom that she—well, my mom thinks your mom is kinda fixed on him. I mean, more than friendly."

Frankie's throat went tight. "So?"

"Your mom's crazy for you to like him, for you both to get on. I thought you knew."

"Of course I did," Frankie said. "All along."

"Well good, then." Anna pushed her empty sundae cup and reached for her shoulder bag. "Look, can't we drop the whole thing, Frankie? It's not my business who your mom sees or anything. But you know—"

"Know what?"

Anna opened her bag, took out her wallet. Then, as though she'd made up her mind, she looked up and the words tumbled out. "My mom says, well . . . Your mom's neat. And she's not that old. In a few more years, you'll be off into the world, and you can't expect her to stay alone for the rest of her life."

Frankie sucked in her breath to protest.

"Hey," Anna held up a hand. "Cool it. I didn't say she was marrying this guy, though my mom says it looks like. What I'm wondering is, will he come to live with you, or will you move into the city? Either way, you'll be making changes with a new man in the house."

Frankie let her breath out. They'd worked it all out,

hadn't they? Anna, Mrs. Green, and everybody. What Mom was going to do, how they bet Frankie would feel about it, being such a daddy's girl and all, and how she ought to feel, if she was half a daughter. She stood, her chest all tight and funny. Without a word, she turned and pushed her way out. Before she knew it, she was striding the length of the mall, bumping into people, crashing into carts and shopping bags. This is ridiculous, she told herself. I don't mind Mom getting a boyfriend. I even like the guy.

So why was she so riled? Frankie thought she heard Anna call once, but her legs kept up their pace and then she was outside. She reached her street, full speed. It was the not realizing that hurt, she told herself. Anna's jumping her, not giving her a chance to be gracious, to have some control. Whose life was it, anyhow? She felt the total fool. Everybody had known but her: Mom's trips to the beauty parlor, the dresses, the staying late in town. Anna had known, how long since? And had met with Frankie every day, without saying a word! What kind of friend was that? And Mom was no better, bribing Frankie into the city with museum trips to set her up for inspection like a pie on a plate. "People can be so rotten," Frankie muttered, stomping up the front path.

Her mother was in the kitchen, at the stove. "Hi, hon," she called as Frankie strode through the front hall and up the stairs. "You're home early. Muffins on the way. Where's Annie?"

Frankie hit the top landing, and pushed through into her

bedroom. There, she locked her door, threw herself onto the bed, and turned on her radio full blast.

. . .

Hahn stood before the control panel, shaking his head. The ship had repaired itself as much as it was going to. But both drives were damaged beyond repair; the main shaft was shattered. This ship wasn't going to fly again. Ever. He was trapped. All he could do for now was to keep edging forward through time; watching, waiting, hiding in the long grass from his pursuer. . . .

A bell pinged, loud and shrill.

Hahn looked up. The interact alarm had grown brighter, was pulsing more rapidly: the effect of his crash on that little settlement close by the swamp was moving up another notch!

Hahn consulted his chronometer. Four Earth hours, he'd spent in the LSRM, while he and the ship got put to rights. During that short space, the ship had crawled forward . . . he consulted the time gauges . . . fourteen whole years through this world's space/time continuum.

Hahn brought his craft to a halt, called up a replay of his crash sixteen hours earlier—fourteen years ago, for the folk out there. The top boxes filled with holographs of dark clouds reflecting his fiery descent. Hahn watched the recorded crash take him once more over the cluster of hide shelters close to the swamp. He saw now, as he'd not had time to see during the actual crash, the tiny human figures flee into the night as the fireball passed over them. He backed up the pancorder, slowed the replay, boosted the vision enhancer, observed quite clearly the tallest man wave his pointed hickory stick toward the crash site, then behind him to a village tent from which had come a baby's loud squall in the aftermath.

Hahn ran the pancorder on, watched a party headed by that tall man walk to the edge of the swamp and gaze toward the crash site, but not, he also noted, venturing in to investigate. Had those people taken his crash as some kind of omen? Hahn ran the 'corder on, watching the pulse of nights and days mount into months, seasons, years, and the pattern began to emerge. On each anniversary of the crash, the tall man returned to the edge of the swamp, the same child with him—growing rapidly with each passing year.

Hahn shifted the ship on to the thirteenth anniversary of his crash, and there, the group was back, and this time—

He froze the time frame, and inspected the group. Now, the boy was wearing clothes—a rough hide cloak, and tunic and leggings—and his scalp was shaven, save for a stiff crest running from brow to nape. Hahn eyed the boy intently, sensing another, more subtle difference: the lad held himself tall, and straighter even than before, with a pride of bearing unusual in one so young.

He had become a man.

Hahn moved forward another year, then another, to the fifteenth anniversary of his crash. The interact alarm kept flashing rapidly. There was the group again, the boy beside them, fifteen years old now, gazing out over the swamp. But this time, instead of turning away, the tall man nodded, and gestured the boy forward, toward the edge of the marsh.

Shifting the ship on again, Hahn watched the boy strike out into the icy waste, and the men walk away back to their village, leaving one of their number to watch.

The boy stood for a moment or two, then, slipping and falling, he began to make his way deeper and deeper into the deadly marsh. He did not get far. As darkness fell, and the snow swirled thick and fast, the boy, unable to move another step, huddled on an island clump of withered reeds.

Hahn frowned in misgiving. Why, why, *why?* this yearly ritual? And why the sudden change? He scanned the data banks for what would happen if things ran on unchecked—and cried out in dismay. In order to avoid doing harm by taking life, he'd pulled back through time, to this empty waste. But in spite of that, unless he, Hahn, could prevent it, this boy was going to die!

Snowflakes drifted from evening cloud as the Elders halted by the sedge line. Below them, dead reed clumps gleamed bone pale against the sky.

Beside them, the boy shivered, despite his moccasins, and his leggings, and deerskin cloak; and his teeth clicked together like bones. But it was not the cold that made him shiver. Somehow he knew, even before Tallspear asked, and Dreamwalker answered, that at last the time had come.

Talk ceased as the men stared out over the desolation whose name they might not utter. Tallspear turned, as he'd turned every one of these past fourteen years, and asked of Dreamwalker beside him. "Is it time?"

The shaman looked out over the dreary waste of mud and

reed, then up to the sky. For long he stood, until the boy's scalp began to tighten expectantly.

At last Dreamwalker spoke.

"It is time," he said. "Now is the hour when man and spirit meet."

Tallspear turned to the youth.

"You heard. You know what you must do. One will stay here to watch for your return, son of my beloved sister, Shining Leaf." Tallspear raised his hand in salute. "May the Great One go with you, O He That Trails In Fire Across The Starry Heavens."

The boy kept his eyes down, wanting to meet his uncle's gaze, to seek one gleam of the affection, the closeness they'd shared for all his life. But to do so at that moment would be unthinkable: a mark of great disrespect. No matter. Tallspear loved him, and would show it—and pride in him when they led him again from that haunted place.

He turned and started down the bank, only to slip on black slime. He snatched at a nearby reed to steady himself, determined not to lose face before the Elders at this solemn moment, but the reed came up with a sucking sound, and he landed flat on his back. He closed his eyes, the pain of shame washing over him.

But there came no response from behind. He glanced back and saw why. The bank was empty. The Elders had already vanished into the failing light, leaving him to the falling snow, and the spirit of that forbidden place.

He struggled onto his knees, and peered up over the bank to where, he knew, among the bushes beyond, a lookout watched. There was no going back now. Resignedly, he turned from the bank and gave his attention to the icy stretch before him.

It was as silent as it was empty. But that, the boy reassured himself, was only to be expected now, in the dead of the year. When he passed by that place in spring and summer, it was alive with birdsong, and many were the trails of otter and muskrat scoring its boundaries.

But never sign of men. The place had once been called *Swamp Where Reeds Grow For Fishing Baskets,* but now folk called it *Black Swamp That Swallowed Great Falling Fire,* shunning it at Tallspear's command for the fifteen years since Dreamwalker had renamed it.

How did the boy know this, when no one had ever directly said so? How did the round black pebbles at the swamp's edge keep their fine, damp sheen? Not from rain or river, but by the fen's own subtle breath.

In the same indirect way, he had always known that at his birth a great fire had plunged from the night sky to cleave the wetness of the wide black swamp. So violent had been the clash of fire and water that clans had heard it from Sapokanikan to Saperewak; from Aquehonga Manacknong to Konaande Kongh. From that fierce embrace had sprung a thick bright mist, a spirit, they said, the one that now dwelled in the swamp.

He inched forward through the dusk, feeling for solid ground. He stumbled, keeled over, frozen leg sinking up to frozen knee. He pulled out his foot again, minus moccasin. With frigid fingers he clutched at reeds, hauled himself out, his heart racing, onto a soft mud ledge.

It would be hard to tell in any light where to tread. One false step and he'd vanish under the marsh. He went on, dodging from island to island of dead reeds, both feet bare now. And the snow fell faster, swirling in the wind.

Had he come in far enough? He looked back, could see no sign of the bank, or of anything through the evening murk. Far enough, perhaps.

Now he must draw the swamp spirit to him, as Dreamwalker had bidden.

He stood straight, closed his eyes, and tried to compose his mind, but now that he was no longer moving, the shivers began, little surface shivers at first, crawling over his skin like strange snow lice. Then shudders came from ever deeper within his body. His teeth clicked together and he began to moan. Then, after how long he could not tell, the cold, the moaning stopped. His feet and hands, which had lost all feeling, began to grow warm, then hot, so hot that he cried out with the pain of it.

This was no way for a man to behave, he told himself angrily. He clamped his jaws tight on his agony and wrapped his arms about his chest. His head, his sodden cloak—frozen rigid now, were caked in snow, and icicles hung at his throat from his frozen breath. The outside world now seemed unreal: Tallspear, his mother, Dreamwalker, the aromatic warmth of his tent, the village, the planting fields, the fishing grounds beyond. Reality had shrunken to that one small island in the waste. He squatted, closed his eyes, and let his chin fall to his chest.

He came to in alarm.

Hadn't he been taught how to resist the charm of snow-sleep? He must move his body, chafe his frozen limbs. He tried to uncurl, to rise and stretch himself, but could not.

He lifted his head to call upon the spirit of that world, the being born of fire and water the night of his own birth, that it might come and save him. But all he uttered was a feeble moan.

Was Dreamwalker wrong about his birth, after all? If so, then the prophecy was false, and his given name, a lie. And he was good as dead already here, in this place. He stared out into the darkness, fighting stirrings of self-pity. Dead, he'd lie until the crows picked his bones, for who would venture in by one step to retrieve his body? Not Tallspear, nor even Dreamwalker. Not anyone.

He tried to rally. *O Great Swamp Spirit, hear me,* he cried silently. *I am here to meet you, face-to-face, even as Dreamwalker foretold. As you are a great spirit, fetch me out of this deathly cold into your cloud cave, and restore me.*

At a faint, far cry, the boy's lids lifted the merest slit, then opened wide. He blinked rapidly, brushed snow from his face. A point of light shone far out in the blackness; steady and round, not like the wavering flame of a torch. Small, bright as a star, it neared swiftly, through snowflakes flying thick as duck down. He felt his heart beat under his frozen ribs. Yes. Over the sound of the wind came the snap of brittle reeds, the squelch of mud, and the tread of heavy feet.

A massive shape loomed out of the dark and bent toward him—and the bright light burst like a silent ice-flower.

The boy opened his eyes onto darkness, became slowly aware of warmth around him, and a faint humming as of a late bee swarm. He was, he discovered, lying on his back, on bedding softer than straw, or hide, or even the finest feathers. Memory came back slowly: the swamp spirit—he'd called on it to save him from the cold. And that spirit had come, a huge shape bending over him in the snow. Was he even now in the spirit's cloud cave?

He tried to move, but could not. And yet he didn't feel tied down in any way. Was he dead? Was he now a spirit, too?

"Keep still. You're alive and safe, and getting well. Just lie and rest until you are completely healed."

The spirit—speaking in the village tongue! Once again, the boy struggled, but he couldn't even turn his head.

"Relax," the voice said. "You are in no danger. That's better," it went on, as he let go and lay still. "You'll be out soon."

"Out of what?" the boy demanded. "Why is it so dark?"

"You're in my LSRM—that is, my—my healing canoe.

It feels good, no?'' The voice was not deep like Tallspear's, the boy noticed now. Or harsh, like Dreamwalker's, but higher, and mild as any mother's.

Encouraged, the youth spoke up. ''You're the swamp spirit.''

''I'm no spirit: I'm Hahn.''

Hahn? The boy's heart beat faster. This being, this ''Hahn'' not a spirit—*the* spirit, of the swamp? Not so, he reasoned doggedly. Who or what else would hear one's very thought? No, this Hahn was indeed spirit, and a devious one. What was the purpose of denying it? Perhaps—yes, perhaps, he thought, this spirit, knowing who he was, and his purpose, was testing him. In which case, the boy resolved, it were wise to hold his tongue until he saw which way the wind blew.

Silence followed, filled only with the humming.

The silence lengthened.

''I say again: I mean you no harm,'' Hahn-spirit said at last. ''You were nearly dead out there. So I brought you back and put you in the LS—the healing canoe. As you can tell you're nearly good as new again. A while more and you'll be on your way. So now: how would you pass the time? Should you and I talk? I myself would very much like that.''

The boy tried once more to move, and failed.

''You're still not sure of me, I see. I repeat, I'm not, as you think, one of your spirits. I'm just a visitor here.''

Visitor? This being who'd dwelt in the swamp for full fifteen years without showing himself? That was not how visitors behaved. They came with great noise, bearing many gifts, and made much speech with the village Elders. No, whatever this Hahn said, he was a spirit, the spirit of this place. Yet, not a bad one, for even now the boy was aware of comfortable warmth, of the absence of pain, and, come to think of it, of hunger and thirst. "How long have I been in here?"

"One-and-a-half days. Your folk left you out there to die for reasons best known to them. If I hadn't seen it, you'd be dead. In fact, you almost were, young brave."

One-and-a-half days? The boy frowned up into the darkness.

"Why? Why did they leave you?"

Now the boy was puzzled. If—as it seemed—Dreamwalker was right, and he and this swamp spirit had been destined to meet, then the spirit would know that, surely. If not, one might not tell; might not utter the secret, the forbidden truths: the purpose of his mission, and a dead ancestor's name.

"I begin to see a little, young brave," Hahn-spirit said, as though the boy had actually spoken. "What is in your mind you may not voice aloud. Well, you don't have to. Just think what you would say, and I will listen."

"How?" The boy cried triumphantly. "If you're not spirit, how can you reach into my mind and hear my thought?"

"Well said." Hahn-spirit sounded impressed. "You might not feel it, but there's a cap on your head. Through its . . . magic, as you would call it, your thought passes from your mind across into mine, clear as your spoken voice. So think away now, please, and tell me what I must learn."

Think away? Did this Hahn take him for a fool, to trick him into believing spirit was merely magician? The boy's brow creased. Things were not going right. He was supposed to meet the swamp spirit as a man, face-to-face, not speak to him lying in the dark, like a captive beast.

"Your mind seems troubled, young brave. What is the matter?"

The boy remained silent.

"Please—trust me," Hahn-spirit said at last. "You must, if I'm to help you and put things right."

The boy considered. He didn't understand all this spirit said; couldn't fathom what was going on, but there was something in that voice that made the boy decide to trust him. "All right." The boy closed his eyes, opened his mind, and let the thoughts flow forth. His head began to buzz. His mind blurred. Tiny points of light glistened above him, bright as raindrops in full sun. They flared, flashed, then dissolved into mist, which rolled and thundered across his vision like the waves of the great o jik̆ ha dä gé ga.

Was he now asleep, or did he dream? The Hahn-spirit's voice murmured in his ear: low, and soothing; soft as the dove's in summer.

"A . . . ha, now I hear you, and begin to understand. You come from the village of the Little Hill, young brave, on the island of Manahata, Manachatas, Manhattan. Your clan is Manates, of Upper Delaware. You eat the flesh of deer, fish from the Mahicanituk, and maize from your planting fields. Your village is small, smaller than Sapokanikan and Kon-aande Kongh. And your fields are tiny. Yet your people are fierce, and no man picks quarrel with them lightly. Yesterday I came into this place. One-and-a-half days only have passed for me since I landed, fifteen years for you. During all those years no man has set foot in this swamp, although each year at this time you were brought to its edge and taken away. Why? And why did they leave you this time? Aa . . . ah, I sense your withdrawal. Listen: I appreciate your concern, but you have nothing to fear. I swear none of what you say is really coming out aloud, even though, as I said before, it sounds like it. Only think of what you would say to me, and I will hear."

The boy released a long, quiet breath, and sent out his thought. *Surely you know all this. Dreamwalker and the Elders brought me here each year to meet you. But every year he said that it was not yet time. Until now. This year, he said that the moment had come. And he was right, for here I am.*

"But why, young brave? Why are we to meet? And why now?"

The boy sounded perplexed. *Because of your coming, and because of my mother's uncle, whose name one may not utter aloud: Firecloud, He Who Strides In Fiery Cloud Across the Night Sky.*

"Why not speak his name aloud?"

One never speaks of those who have passed to other regions.

"Oh."

They think I am he come again—he, the greatest soul ever to live among my clan! For all the many moons since his departing, my folk have hoped for his return.

"Hmmm. Why do they think you're his reincarnation?"

When he was born, a star fell to earth. Likewise at my

birth, a trail of fire fell from the heavens—the fire of your coming.

The boy heard a long, low groan. Had he caused this being pain?

"It's as I feared," Hahn-spirit murmured, as though to himself. "The very worst has happened, as if I had not enough trouble already! What am I to do? How can I put this right?"

The spirit sounded worried, more worried than he should, the boy thought. Surely Hahn didn't expect him to answer? He held his peace, waiting for the spirit to go on.

"What do you think, young brave?" Hahn-spirit said at last. "Are you the great one reincarnate? You don't sound so sure. What if I sent you back, with the message that they were mistaken?"

Dreamwalker never lies. And he never makes mistakes. As for me, I don't know. Oh, I'm brave as any other man, but I don't feel great. Firecloud was a brave, so, likewise, am I. Like him I wear the crest of warrior. And one day, so they hold, I shall be sachem also, and lead my people. Two years ago, at the time of huskanaw, this made me glad and proud. Dreamwalker pronounced me the One Who Is He Come Again; named me He Who Trails In Fire Across The Starry Heavens, on account of Firecloud, and the fiery omen at my birth.

" 'He Who Trails In Fire Across the Starry Heavens'? Hmmm. A good name. But overly long, even for me, and I've come across all kinds, in my time. I'll call you Sky-fire-trail, if you don't mind."

Sky-fire-trail . . . The name sounded most strange in the boy's ears, yet he respectfully said nothing, accepting it as a mark of the swamp spirit's singular favor.

"Well, Sky-fire-trail: how does being great feel now?"

I'm not sure. Out there just now I felt as powerful as the mosquito at the first frost. But now, well. Perhaps I can tell you better when we have talked more.

"Talked about what?"

Sky-fire-trail frowned in the closed, dark space. Again he thought: surely that one would know? Agh, Hahn-spirit was no doubt still testing him. *Dreamwalker says that you descended in fire at my birth to warn us of some great calamity that is coming upon the clan. What it is, not even he can say. Only you, the great swamp spirit, can reveal it. Dreamwalker says, and to me only, for I am the one who will deliver us from this thing.*

"You are?" Hahn-spirit didn't sound so certain. "What gives you that idea?"

Sky-fire-trail frowned. Was this more testing still? *After my trial at huskanaw, I—and Dreamwalker—saw that it must be so.*

"How? How did you see?"

I who was to celebrate muskrat's dive to the sea floor actually became as he: during my dive to the bottom of the Mahicanituk he and I were one. Muskrat, who, as you must surely know, brought up a handful of mud from the floor of the ocean which he set on turtle's back, and so the world began.

"He did? You did?" Hahn-spirit didn't sound too happy.

So whatever is to happen to our people, only I can prevent it, Dreamwalker said, after I told him of my vision. And now you will tell me what is the calamity, and what I must do.

Another silence, which stretched so long that Sky-fire-trail began to drift into sleep. But as the boy was almost gone, the soft voice came at last. "I regret I cannot help, young brave. As I said, I'm no spirit. And prophecy is not my calling."

Hahn looked down at the LSRM in which the boy now slept, trying to decide. Having crashed, having caused these people to take his coming for a sign, he had from that point on altered their path through history. All he knew so far was that had he, Hahn, not gone out to retrieve that young boy, the altered path would have brought about that young boy's death. Well, now he had prevented it—a major correction, surely?

But not enough, for the interact alarm was still going strong. So whatever the change was, it would go on. Was there no way of putting things all the way back to where they'd been before his crash?

Perhaps if he returned the boy to the edge of the swamp, with some kind of message to let things die down. . . . What message? Hahn sighed again. He hadn't the faintest idea. The boy said the shaman never made mistakes, never told lies. And face it, the man's prediction had fulfilled itself! To send the boy back with some crude rationalization would be insulting beyond words—neither would it work.

Traveling the galaxies, Hahn had learned to respect the different ways that thinking creatures used to find out truth. He must respect this shaman. Must give him credit for what he said. Suppose something bad lay in this people's future?

He, Hahn, had somehow gotten entangled in it all. He looked at his chronometer. Time was wasting. Whatever he chose to do, he must get the boy out of here, back to his people. Now, while Sky-fire-trail slept, he'd go out and set flares to mark a safe path out of the swamp.

Hahn went to the back wall, and from one of the lockers slid out a tray of loose crystals; remote controls that could govern the ship from outside. He picked out a red one and a blue one, and stowed them in his leggings. Then he took up a lump of white quartz and weighed it in his hand. This crystal could transmat him anywhere he wished through space and time. Thus it served as ship's door.

Pocketing his time stone, Hahn took out a pack of flares from another door in the storage wall. Then he secured the ship's controls, set the perimeter alarms. If the enemy neared, Hahn could be back in a nanosecond. He checked the LSRM. The boy would sleep for another hour or so, when the lid was set to open, by which time Hahn should be back.

Hahn closed his hand about the time stone, and shut his eyes. His shape began to darken, then fade into shadow, and a moment later, he was gone.

. . .

Tuesday, Frankie received a package from Florida. She took it upstairs, sat cross-legged on her bed, opened it. The book that Dad had promised her. She took it from the wrapper, and looked at the cover. *Mind Children: The Future of Robot and Human Intelligence,* it was called. By Hans Moravec, the director of the Mobile Robot Laboratory of Carnegie-Mellon University.

Mind children.

Frankie liked the sound of that. She skimmed through the pages, dipping in a little here and there, until a particular paragraph caught her eye.

"Encoded in the large, highly evolved sensory and motor portions of the human brain is a billion years of experience about the nature of the world and how to survive in it. The deliberate process we call reasoning is, I believe, the thinnest veneer of human thought, effective only because it is supported by this much older and much more powerful, though usually unconscious, sensorimotor knowledge."

She set the book down, looked up sensorimotor. "Both sensory and motor," her Webster said. She read the passage again, slowly. The man was saying, it seemed to her, that while a robot brain might find, say, the square root of two million, four hundred thousand and twenty-eight in a zip, it couldn't do a simple thing like boil water without getting scalded. Or be scared of the dark. Or, maybe, while it might scan, even memorize the whole of Macbeth in sixty seconds flat, it might never *feel* as the characters felt. This fund of human experience and emotion, handed down through the generations: this interface of mind and body—would this distinguish real humans from manufactured ones? She propped her elbows on her knees, getting deeper into thought. No. Not if they gave that mind a body cloned from human cells! She sat up excitedly. Because those cells, surely, would carry the genetic memories of previous generations in their DNA? Far out! But maybe not too far off. Weren't they talking in the museum show about new advances in cloning techniques? She wished she knew more about it. Dad would know, especially if he'd gotten into this field. She resolved to start reading the book, compiling questions as she went to ask him next time she called Florida.

"Frankie! Tea's up! Come on!"

She closed the book and went downstairs.

"What was the package, Frankie?" Mom set a plate in front of her: chops, mashed potatoes, and a stack of brussels sprouts. Only Mom knew how to spoil a good meal.

Frankie picked up her fork.

"A book from Dad. On artificial intelligence." She might as well say it straight out, to save Mom asking.

"Huh! Isn't there anything he's not into?"

Frankie kept quiet, as she always did when the subject of Dad came up. She thought of purely artificial minds, cool and free of human clutter. "Imagine: a brilliant brain, straight A's, never a black mark, and no parent to nag you to death, or load your plate with stuff that makes you gag."

"Ah," Mom said, catching on, "but then you wouldn't be human."

Frankie eyed her mother thoughtfully across the table. *Human.* She jabbed her fork into her chop. And went to thinking again what a purely artificial robot—an android—would need to make it more human? It certainly would need living parts to make it a *cyborg.* A flesh-and-blood body, made from human cells, for sure. Then it would need to gather human experience. To go outside the lab walls and move and feel and see and hear. Even if it had been strictly programmed only for one single function, such as zapping rivets into cars, or data processing, its biological nature would surely break out at last? If allowed to be with people on a regular basis, at some stage it must start to feel human? She pictured a cyborg breaking from its cell, not some gross, malformed thing like Frankenstein's monster, but, well, a baby under its grown-up exterior, hatching from its egg and going off to, what? Sail a boat, taste good food, laugh at a movie, make friends, fall in love . . .

Her mother cut through her thought.

"Frankie, what's happened with you and Anna? Have you two quarreled?"

Frankie shrugged.

"Oh, Frankie! What about?"

"Nothing. Mom—just leave it, okay?" She snatched up her half-empty plate and made for the sink.

Mom sighed. "Okay. Oh," she said then, as though she'd just thought. "Guess what."

Frankie turned back.

"We're invited to a party in the city Saturday night. I thought we'd make a weekend of it. I'll meet you at Penn Station Friday after your karate lesson—Mrs. Green can take you to the train. We'll stay in a nice hotel near Central Park. Do anything you want all day Saturday. Then we go to the party at night. Come home Sunday first thing. What do you say?"

"Whose party?"

"Dr. Webb's. Isn't it nice of him to invite us?"

"I guess."

As soon as she could, Frankie escaped to her room, feeling all rattled up again. Did Anna know about this jaunt too? Frankie couldn't guess; they hadn't spoken these past two days. She stood in front of her dresser mirror, confronting her irritation. She should go back down, tell her mother it was okay with Frankie if she wanted to take up with a boyfriend, only would she stop pussyfooting around, and let her own daughter in on it *before* she told the entire neighborhood?

Frankie turned from her reflection. That wasn't all of it. But what the rest was, she couldn't say right now, because she didn't know. She took the snapshots of Dad from her bureau drawer. He'd been straight with her, all along, about Edie, that is. She climbed onto her bed, sat herself as usual, and fanned the pictures onto the bedcover. Admit it, it must have been easier for him, telling her from a distance. Frankie tried to put herself in her mother's place, couldn't make it, quite. She sighed. She was glad Mom had a boyfriend.

But marry him?

Since Dad left, she and Mom had settled into a comfortable routine, getting along, for the most part.

Will he come to live with you, I wonder, or will you move into the city? . . . Either way, you'll be making changes with a new man in the house.

She leaned back on her pillows. Face it, Frankie, she thought. You're scared. Her whole world was shifting, and the comfortable and familiar pattern of her life up till now was melting away.

She thought of the kids in the Indian village. Okay, they'd had it rough, but life had been simple then. Hunting deer, fishing, growing corn and tobacco. Eating, sleeping, hanging out. That huskanaw stuff was a breeze, compared with what she was going through. She could just see whoever now, diving as she'd done, and coming up a hero, everybody patting him on the back and calling him one great guy. You could run a rope around his world, mark the inside, and the out. Nothing much would change, for a kid back then. The guy with the huskanaw, she pictured him standing there, beside the bed, arms folded, looking smug.

"You think you're so great," she muttered. "You should try slugging it out here."

"You think you're so tough? How would you like to get assimilated?" came the reply.

Frankie sat nonplussed. She'd forgotten about that. She reached over, and pulled out her Webster's. *Assemble . . . assert . . . assess . . . assets . . . assign . . .* Her finger moved slowly down the page until she found it: *Assimilate: v.t. to make similar or like: to convert into a like substance, as food in the body.* Frankie made a face and read on. *v.i. to become like: to be incorporated in—*

Frankie slammed the book shut.

How would you like to get assimilated?

She pictured the village, and all those harmless people, just going about their business and then—well, now you wouldn't know they'd ever been, except for the names. Their homes, their way of life . . . all swallowed up. . . . Had they simply changed? Or died out? She bit her lower lip thoughtfully. Wasn't it the same thing?

She gazed about her familiar room, trying to imagine how she'd feel, newcomers barging in on her here in Valley Stream, pushing her and Mom out onto the street, knocking down these walls to build some new kind of place for themselves, like that fancy futuristic city in the space show. Or she and Mom, herded into the street with all the neighbors, while giant alien machines like in "War of the Worlds" leveled the houses and shoveled them away.

She pictured herself, running after, shouting, "But what about us? What do we do, where do we go now?" And a cold, metallic voice coming from inside the nearest machine. "Put up or shut up; now make way—you're history!"

Frankie shuddered. Her imaginary brave just now: had his folks died out, or just . . . faded into the scene? Frankie gathered up her pictures. Did it matter? It hadn't happened in his lifetime, he can't have known . . . so what was his beef?

She thought uncomfortably of the exhibits in the Whole Earth Show, the devastated forests, the dying seas. Could be happening to her world, could be starting now, right under their noses, and not enough being done about it.

She looked around her room, as though seeing it for the first time. Never mind the world outside, what about this one; here, within the walls of this house?

. . . you'll be making changes . . .

Getting assimilated into the new order of things.

Frankie took up a shot of Dad taken on Long Beach in the act of catching her beachball. He was smiling, squinting into the sun. She looked from him to herself in the mirror. People said how like Mom she was, but she was just as much like Dad. Actually, Mom and Dad could be brother and sister, same build, almost the same height—when Mom wasn't wearing heels. Same dark skin, dark eyes, and blue-black hair.

Dad. She held the snapshot to her cheek. What would he think of Mom's new boyfriend? Should she call him, let him know? Better not. It was Mom's affair. Besides, it might be premature, all this talk about Mom and Webb getting married, and all. If the relationship fell through, wouldn't that be one in the eye for Anna dear and Mrs. Green? "Don't get me wrong," she whispered, looking into her father's smiling eyes. "I'm happy for you, and Edie, and everything. And I'm used to things now, at least, most of the time. But this with Mom—it's so sudden, and a whole new situation to think about, and I'm scared, I know you'll understand. . . ."

Bingham Webb? She kissed her father's picture. *However nice he is, he never will be you!*

. . .

When Sky-fire-trail came to, the healing canoe cover was lifted back, and light bright and hot as the sun shone down upon him. "Hahn-spirit?" He shaded his eyes against the glare and called again.

There was no reply.

He drew up his knees, gripped the edge of the healing canoe, sat up without the slightest stiffness or effort, and looked about. The cloud cave was, he saw, quite small, and curved like the inside of a silver eggshell, studded with tiny colored lights thick as mussels on the rock shore.

He looked down. His body, naked but for his breech clout, was draped with the same kind of silver stuff that lined the canoe. Smooth, shiny, and so feather-light he couldn't feel it on his skin. He raised his hands, examined them, but could see no signs of red or swelling.

Sky-fire-trail carefully climbed down to the floor. All that time he'd lain in there, really sick, so Hahn-spirit said. And, indeed, Sky-fire-trail well knew what bitter cold did to a man who stayed out too long and still. Had felt the beginnings of it in him that night out on the swamp. But he didn't feel in the least bit sick now.

The floor was warm under the soles of his feet. Adjusting to the general brightness, he turned and turned about in awe. So many marvels in that place to see all at once, but his gaze was caught and held by the multitudes of tiny lights: sparkling stones embedded in the cave walls—red, yellow, blue, purple, green, orange—all the colors of the rainbow. He reached out to touch one, but at the last moment, he lowered his hand. The stones belonged to Hahn-spirit. Who knew what power rested in them?

He turned about to see a whole pile of loose stones heaped on a tray half-out of one wall. He went over, eyeing them intently. Different sizes, and colors, just like the others, heaped like gathered shells on the sand. He was just taking one up between finger and thumb, when the air beside him swirled and wavered as on a warm spring day. A mist cloud formed, and out of it a voice cried: "Don't touch those stones!"

The cloud darkened, condensed, and Sky-fire-trail saw Hahn-spirit clearly for the first time. He was so *big,* the boy thought, in surprise. A veritable giant! Sky-fire-trail had expected a smaller being—perhaps on account of the gentle voice that had calmed and soothed him in the darkness of the healing canoe. But tall as he was himself, Sky-fire-trail reached but to Hahn-spirit's broad shoulders. From there on down, the large body was encased in strange, dark blue stuff, tunic and leggings all in one; with bright red sleeves.

And the head? The strong and bony skull was covered in dark, stubbled hair, rather like Sky-fire-trail's own, only lacking the brave's crest. But the face! The eyes that watched him, the boy had never seen such, were round and blue as the chicory flower. The nose was large and straight as a peg; the mouth, wide and full—though looking severely now; while the skin was yet smooth and polished as a child's. So this was what a spirit looked like?

Sky-fire-trail stood his ground, drew himself up to his full height and saluted. "Hahn-spirit."

"Hahn." The being advanced on Sky-fire-trail, pushing him back a full step but all he did then was to open his large palm to reveal a white crystal big as a robin's egg, and hold it out over the tray.

"Well, young brave? And what did you think to do with these things?"

Sky-fire-trail ignored the question, all fired up with his own. "You said you're not spirit. Yet you come and go just as Dreamwalker said, like the gray mist over the swamp."

The blue eyes looked mildly. "I don't do the coming and going. This does." He held the crystal to the light, and as he did so, it flashed with a brief, fierce fire of its own.

Sky-fire-trail nodded first to it, then to the pile on the tray. "What is it, what are they?"

"They're . . ." The spirit seemed at a loss. "They're . . . my stones-that-work-at-a-distance."

"Work what? At a distance from what? I don't understand."

"Of course not." Hahn-spirit waved his arm about. "All this is a big boat. *Ship*. It moves through space and time. When I'm here," he pointed to the stones embedded in the walls, "those work the ship for me." He drew two more stones from his leggings: one, red; the other, the color of his eyes, and cupped them in his palm with the white one. "But when I leave the ship and go outside, I take these with me, to operate the ship—to tell it what to do—from wherever I happen to be." He held up the red crystal. "This one starts the ship. And this—'' He dropped it and took up the blue one—''brings it to me—as you would whistle to summon a horse.''

''Horse?'' The word meant nothing to Sky-fire-trail. ''What is 'horse'?''

Hahn briefly closed his eyes, as though thinking, then opened them again. ''Oh, I see you don't have the creature yet.'' He raised his hand shoulder high, palm down. ''It's an animal about so big that you will ride one day. Now, say you're here, and the horse is a way off: call or whistle and it will come to you. Well, through this stone, when I'm outside I can call this ship to me. Do you follow?''

Sky-fire-trail nodded doubtfully.

''Good, then.'' Hahn-spirit set the crystals on the pile, wiped his hands over his blue coverings, and made to slide the tray back into the wall.

''Wait.'' Sky-fire-trail caught his arm, pointing to the white crystal. ''Say what that one does.''

''My time stone? I'm not sure you'd understand,'' Hahn said.

''Then I shall guess. By its means you come and go as the mist, in and out of the ship, which has no door that I can see.''

Hahn-spirit looked startled, then pleased, as Dreamwalker did whenever Sky-fire-trail found him roots that he sought. ''You could say that.''

''I guess further: if you're not spirit, and it is truly the stone that makes you come and go, then it would make me come and go also.''

Hahn-spirit looked startled. Then he laughed. "You, my brave, will one day make a fine, wise sachem." He slid the tray away now, and turned briskly to rows of small holes in the wall behind him in which light and shadow flickered.

Sky-fire-trail leaned forward, curious. He saw now that the holes were small boxes, apparently open to the room. He tried to reach into one, only to bang his knuckles against some unseen force. He peered into them, trying to make sense of what he saw.

"What are these?"

Hahn smiled. "Holoboxes. Right now they're set on visual scan, that is, they're working as scanners—monitors."

"Scanners? Monitors?"

"Lookouts—scouts—extra eyes, then. They show any part of the swamp I want to see. Like the trail you came in by."

Scouts? Eyes? Sky-fire-trail looked at the monitors, thinking that they were not shaped like any scouts or eyes that he had ever seen.

Hahn-spirit directed Sky-fire-trail's gaze to a box on the top row. "What do you see?"

Peering in, Sky-fire-trail saw only strange smudges, like smoke.

"It's hard, making sense of moving pictures for the first time." Hahn pointed. "That dark patch is the clump of bushes on top of the bank where your uncle set his men to watch for you. Do you see now?"

Sky-fire-trail stared blankly. Then all at once, he saw not

only the bushes, but that the strip of shadow below them formed the bank at the swamp's edge, and that the darkness overall was the night sky above it.

As he watched, there was movement, and a strange glowing shape emerged from the bushes. He frowned, struggled to focus, then leapt back in alarm. It was a tiny human figure: Tallspear's lookout—and all in flames!

"You're a hunter! That is a wall of cages! You trap us, and shut us up, and burn us!" Sky-fire-trail backed up against the wall, casting about wildly for a way to escape before he, too, was caught and set alight.

Hahn shook his head. "I'm no hunter. It's night. The boxes are set on infrared—" He broke off, then tried again. "They're set to catch the heat coming off a person's body and show it as a glow in the dark." He spread his great hands in appeal. "Look, if I'd want to harm anyone, I've have done it long since." He smiled suddenly, showing big, white teeth, not one missing. "As it is—oh, here I am, forgetting. You've been up for quite a while. You must need recharging. You are hungry, no?"

Hungry? The boy felt the growling in his middle and nodded. Truly this Hahn seemed to know his wants better than he did himself—but then, was he not a spirit?

Hahn went to the tray wall, and pressed several crystals in rapid succession. With a short, sharp buzz, a door opened, revealing a small cavity. From this cavity, Hahn withdrew a bowl unlike any Sky-fire-trail had seen before. It was white, and shiny, and light as basswood.

In the bowl were small pellets, grayish green. Sky-fire-trail dashed the bowl away, scattering the pellets. "What do you think me, that you give me rabbit turds to eat!"

Hahn retrieved a pellet and popped it in his mouth. "They're not turds, but something much better. What is your favorite dish?"

Sky-fire-trail considered. "Fish," he said suspiciously. "Fresh from the Mahicanituk, the Shatemuc."

"Quite so." Hahn-spirit picked up another pellet, held it out. "Here. Try this."

Sky-fire-trail took it, put it on his tongue. For a moment, the tiny thing lay there, dry, and tasteless. Then suddenly, it swelled, filling his mouth and he tasted fish, felt moist, firm flakes of it separating out under his palate. His eyes gleamed. He might well be eating a fish not only just caught, but fresh baked over the smoky fire just the way he liked it.

He bit down and chewed. And while he chewed, he bent for another pellet, then another, and another. As he ate, he looked around.

"This space ship: where does it come from?"

Hahn-spirit pointed up.

"From the sky?"

"From the stars."

The stars! "Will you one day go back there?"

"I hope so."

"When?"

Hahn-spirit shrugged.

"Why did you come here?"

Hahn-spirit glanced to the boxes, as he did constantly. "It's quiet."

Sky-fire-trail thought he understood. "Someone hunts you. There is bad blood between you."

"Yes." Hahn turned his great blue eyes on him and they both smiled, pleased with their mutual understanding.

"That one must be powerful, to put you to flight. A brother spirit. Why does he hunt you?"

"I wish I knew, exactly. My guess is he'd harm what I protect."

"If he comes, will you fight?"

"Alas, no, young brave. Not here, at any rate, I'm sorry to disappoint you. My function is to foster life; I'm forbidden to do anything that would harm this place. I'd simply leave, fast, to find another hiding place."

"What! With me here?"

Hahn shook his head solemnly. "I'd put you back on your mud-pile—so pray he doesn't sniff me out until you've finished your fish."

Sky-fire-trail picked up the last pellet.

"More?" Hahn asked him, his hand going to the wall. Sky-fire-trail shook his head. "Water."

In seconds Hahn produced water by the same magic, in a cup not of clay, but of the same light, white stuff as the bowl.

Sky-fire-trail sniffed, smelled nothing. He tipped the cup, sipped, then drained it in one thirsty draught. The water was cold, with a sharp tang unlike the water from the village spring. He wiped his mouth with the back of his hand and gave the cup back. "I'm going now," he said.

"Wait." Hahn glanced up doubtfully to a bright red crystal

flashing in the wall. "You haven't yet gotten what you came for."

Sky-fire-trail's eyes narrowed. "You said you had no visions to show me. That you're not spirit, but visitor."

"That was then. I've been thinking. Let me get this straight: I'm supposed to show you some calamity that's coming to your people, right?"

"Yes." Sky-fire-trail watched Hahn-spirit narrowly, sensing some plan here, some hidden purpose in that one's mind.

"Well, I think I've seen it. You're sure you want to?"

"Yes!"

"Then you shall. But first—" Hahn-spirit went to the tray wall, slid aside a panel, and drew from behind it a black cloth headband encrusted in tiny crystal beads that sparkled like hoarfrost under the light.

"Here, put this on."

Sky-fire-trail took it, turned it about. "What is this?"

"A universal translator. Band-of-many-tongues," Hahn-spirit said.

Sky-fire-trail looked to Hahn-spirit's bare brow. "Where's yours?"

"Built-in." Hahn-spirit tapped his temple.

"Built-in?" Was that some jest perhaps? Hahn-spirit was smiling, but then he almost always was. Sky-fire-trail slipped the band on warily, set it over his forehead. He felt a slight prickle, then warmth. Then nothing. He raised his hand, traced the band's shape, stark against his shaven skull. Yes, it was there.

"Now . . ." Hahn-spirit bent down, rummaged around

near the bottom of the wall, found a larger hole, and pulled out a neat-folded pile. "Your clothes."

Leggings, tunic, and lost moccasins, fully restored—everything but his deerskin cloak. Sky-fire-trail put them on, and at once began to grow uncomfortably hot in that little chamber.

"Ah, but it's fit to freeze a Legumiaan flame-bird outside," Hahn said.

"Pardon?"

Hahn lightly smacked his temple. "A—a phoenix? Thunderbird! Or is that only out West? Never mind, the point is that it's cold, so wear this." Hahn picked up the silver blanket from the healing canoe and held it out.

Sky-fire-trail took it and threw it over one shoulder, tied it at his opposite hip, after the manner of Tallspear, then glanced at his reflection in the wall. He looked fine, in the god-blanket and the band-of-many tongues. If only the Elders could see him now! He drew himself up proudly.

But as Hahn-spirit took out the time stone, Sky-fire-trail realized that he, too, was about to dissolve as the mist over the swamp. Would he feel it? Would there be pain? "How do you work the magic?"

"Quite simply, young brave," Hahn-spirit said, "I hold it, so. Then I picture where I'm going. Don't worry," he added, as though Sky-fire-trail had spoken his concern out loud. "It won't hurt, though when we move you'll feel a tingling, and you might even feel giddy, for a bit, even after we're there. And likely you'll see stars. But there's no harm."

Sky-fire-trail listened, wondering where they were going,

thinking of the calamity he'd find there. He adjusted the blanket about him.

Hahn-spirit was watching. ''Still want to go?''

''Yes.''

''Very well. One last word: while we're moving, on no account let go of me, or you'll be lost and I might not be able to find you. And when we arrive, stay by me and do exactly as I say. Those who travel by this stone must see and not be seen. That is the law, understand?''

Sky-fire-trail nodded again. He well knew ''must'' and ''law.''

Hahn-spirit took Sky-fire-trail's arm, and closed his eyes.

Sky-fire-trail regarded him dubiously. Must he now close his eyes also? And open them on what? ''This calamity—''

Hahn-spirit looked down. ''Trust me; now close your eyes.''

Sky-fire-trail obeyed.

All at once there came a terrifying crackling as of a forest fire raging about them. The calamity? He grew so afraid, he almost broke free and ran. But Hahn-spirit had warned him to keep hold. Sky-fire-trail took a deep breath. Was he not a brave? A brave feared nothing. He blew the fear from his body and held on.

They traveled long. Noises came and went. A wind sprang up. Gasping for breath, his hair, his god-blanket streaming behind him, Sky-fire-trail felt his fear rise again and again, but each time, perhaps guessing his thought, Hahn-spirit tightened grip to reassure him. At last the wind slowed, the noises lessened, and Hahn-spirit whispered for him to open his eyes.

They stood among thick bushes under broad sunlight. As close as Sky-fire-trail could guess, it was near noon on a late summer day.

His finger to his lips, Hahn-spirit drew Sky-fire-trail forward through the bushes and parted them. Sky-fire-trail went quite still. The bushes stood back from a wide, straight, stony trail. On either side of that trail reared walls to a height of at least four men. These walls were made of wood and baked clay. Brick, Hahn called it. They were also pierced with rows of holes like Hahn-spirit's strange eye-boxes, only bigger, and they shone in the sunlight.

Sky-fire-trail stared at the people now going along by the walls, and crossing from one side of the trail to the other. They were pale-skinned as Hahn-spirit, and they were draped from head to toe, not in skin of buck and doe, but strange stuffs of all colors. Were these people spirits also?

A loud clatter started behind him, making Sky-fire-trail jump. Coming down the trail was a large cage pulled by two strange black beasts with crests of long black hair, and tails.

Was this the calamity?

Sky-fire-trail tried to pull free, to go to meet it, face-to-face, but Hahn-spirit tightened his hold. "Those are the horses I told you about. Be still, young brave."

The moving cage was almost upon them when it stopped with much bouncing and creaking. A small flap opened in the cage's side, and two people stepped down: a man and woman, the woman draped in heavy stuffs down to the ground.

The man walked to the nearest wall and banged it with his stick. Then he stood shifting from one foot to the other. People passed him, to and fro. An opening suddenly appeared in the wall, and the man and woman went through.

''What is this? Where are we?''

''We're standing just where we were,'' Hahn-spirit murmured. ''Only we're many, many moons away, in your great-great-great-great grandchildren's time. Those boxes are called houses,'' he added. ''Dwellings for these people who walk the trail. Those holes are called windows, and their purpose is to let in light and air.''

Stunned, Sky-fire-trail looked to the earth beneath his feet, to the tall buildings of wood and clay, and the many people bustling past, more numerous than all the people of his village. This—the middle of the swamp? ''Where is the swamp? Who are they? Spirits like you?''

Hahn-spirit shook his head. ''No, young brave. They are, like you, just people of this world, only of another time.''

''I do not understand.''

A knot of boys burst onto the trail with raucous shouts, and raced toward the bushes, boys with the same pale faces, and strange clothes.

''Quick,'' Hahn said. ''They mustn't see us. Shut your eyes and hold on.''

The children burst through the bushes. Sky-fire-trail had one glimpse of a startled face a bare stone's throw from him, then his head began to spin and he was forced to shut his eyes.

Where to now? Or, rather, *when?* On they went, Sky-fire-trail clutching Hahn's arm tightly, while noises started up around them. The farther they traveled, the louder the noises grew until there was a bewildering clamor of shouts, and bellows as of angry beasts; distant whistles, clangings, and the murmurs, the cries, the roar of many clans on one great warpath.

Hahn-spirit released him. The journey was over, but Sky-fire-trail, his eyes still closed, put his hands over his ears to shut out the din. Where was he now? Very far from home, for sure.

Sky-fire-trail opened his eyes, and found himself standing in deep shadow. From what? At first, he could make no sense of what he saw. He stared about him, then up, and up . . . and up. The brick walls were gone, replaced by immense stone bluffs that soared into the evening haze, their tops dazzling against a tiny patch of sky.

"Remember those other dwellings? This is what they've become. They're called skyscrapers. Come on. Remember: we must see but not be seen."

Sky-fire-trail stayed gazing upward, shocked. Dwellings? For how many? And of what manner of people, presuming to offer such bold insult to the gods? To raise such walls in stark defiance of the natural laws? Scandalized, Sky-fire-trail padded after Hahn-spirit toward the cacophony beyond.

People milled through narrow sunlit space thicker than leaves on a tree, more numerous than trees in the forest; teemed like fish spawn in the estuary, termites on a rotten log. Pale people, dark people, bodies of all colors and sizes, wearing stranger stuffs. He leapt back at a sudden trumpeting, dropped into hunter's crouch, drawing his small stone knife, ready for trouble. The noise grew, the crowd scattered as a fierce yellow beast tore through at great speed, its eyes flashing, its voice letting out a loud bellow.

He watched, unmoving, until the crowds had closed in its wake, like a herd of wandering deer after the wolf is past. "That beast is the calamity?"

Hahn made a wry face. "You could say that. But it's not a beast. It's a *taxi*. People ride it from place to place."

Sky-fire-trail straightened slowly. *Taxi*. Yes, bold folk to rear such godless piles, and to ride such fierce creatures.

"Where is the calamity?"

"I'm afraid it is here, all about us, young brave."

Sky-fire-trail looked at Hahn-spirit, frowning. "I do not see," he began, and then he did, and he straightened slowly. "Still we stand on the same spot." He looked out past Hahn-spirit's shoulder at the space behind him, to a world become crazed, or something worse for which he had no name.

"What happened to the swamp? To my people?"

A sound began deep inside him, tore up with great force into his throat. Drawing back his lips, Sky-fire-trail took a shuddering breath to push it out, but Hahn-spirit, putting a hand over his mouth, pulled him in close.

"Remember the law, Sky-fire-trail. Come on, it's time to go."

The journey back left Sky-fire-trail so weak that he fell to the ship's floor, where he lay, only half-aware of Hahn-spirit pulling out the tray of stones and tossing down the stones-that-work-at-a-distance.

"Are you all right?" Hahn-spirit bent over him anxiously.

Sky-fire-trail couldn't reply. Those people. His mind buckled under the weight of their numbers.

Hahn-spirit brought water from the wall.

Sky-fire-trail took the cup, sipped. "Where we went." He pointed down. "It was this very spot, many moons from now."

"Yes."

"And the swamp? And my people?"

"Gone."

"Gone?" Sky-fire-trail lowered his cup. "Gone where?"

Hahn hesitated. "You really want to know?"

He nodded.

"In the time of your grandchildren many people will come across the o jik̆ ha dä gé ga in many great ships. Over the years, they'll cut down the forests for timber, level hills, drain the swamp. They will prosper and multiply after their own fashion, until they're so numerous they'll have to build upward, to the sky."

"And my people?"

"They'll not be strong enough to withstand them. Their way of life will fail when the trees, the open spaces, are gone. They'll scatter, disappear." Hahn-spirit's large face creased with concern. "It will happen to all of your kind, Sky-fire-trail, the length and breadth of this land. It's ever the same: the few give place to the many, and all in the name of progress."

Sky-fire-trail's brows came together. "It must not be. I'll stop it, somehow."

Hahn-spirit gazed at him, his calm blue eyes clouding

over. When at last he spoke, it seemed to be with great and painful effort. "No, young brave. You cannot. It's already happened, you see."

Sky-fire-trail thought of his quiet village, the fishing waters, the planting fields. Of the other villages, on the island, over the water. Such a dreadful world it was to become. He looked up. He couldn't help his people. But this great swamp spirit could. And must.

"You—Hahn-spirit: you shall stop it for us."

Hahn sighed. "I may not, young brave. Absolutely."

May not? "But you could if you wanted to?"

"It's forbidden, I'm sorry."

Sky-fire-trail stood angrily. "You must help, I shall make you!"

A loud clang broke the quiet. Hahn-spirit leapt up as all around them lights flashed.

"The hunter is here?"

"He sniffs me. Time for you to leave, young brave."

Sky-fire-trail drew back. "I stay."

"Oh, no. It's too dangerous, and, besides, it's against regulations."

A second clang sent Hahn leaping to the boxes. "He's here!"

A bump knocked Sky-fire-trail back against the healing canoe, his head spinning, while all around him the air spat and fizzed with light and sound. Where were they going? Forward, into that terrible future? Or back? Sky-fire-trail looked up, saw streaks of color flashing through the boxes.

"Back!" Hahn shouted. "I'm taking us back, to when your world began!"

When his world began? When muskrat made his dive? Sky-fire-trail pulled himself off the canoe, went to stand beside Hahn-spirit. The ship slowed, and for an instant he saw snatches of empty plain across which lumbered strange beasts with great crests down their spines, while overhead birds with necks longer than a heron's, and clawed wings wider than any eagle's, glided on the winds. The ship speeded up again; more streaks and more colors, faster and faster.

The ship tipped sideways, throwing Sky-fire-trail against the canoe, but Hahn-spirit, braced, stood, watching the monitors, beating strange tattoos on the walls around them. How did that one keep his balance!

Clinging to the canoe, Sky-fire-trail watched the passing display over Hahn's shoulder. On and on the ship went, until Sky-fire-trail began to wonder if they would ever stop. He glanced back over the canoe to the tray wall. The tray of stones was still half-out—and stones lay scattered about the floor. He worked his way around, and, kneeling, he began to gather them up and set them back in their proper place.

He picked up the white quartz, cupped it in his hand. The stone by which Hahn-spirit came and went as the mist over the swamp. . . .

When this chase was over, Hahn-spirit would use this very crystal to put him from the ship. Then Sky-fire-trail's errand would be over, failed. He closed his hand about the stone. If he, Sky-fire-trail, were to take this thing, Hahn-spirit would have to seek him out to get it back. Sky-fire-trail's eyes gleamed. Once out, he'd flee, and keep on fleeing until Hahn-spirit was ready to bargain: the stone in exchange for wiping out the calamity.

In one of the boxes a shape was forming against a black night sky; oval, shining, like a silver egg. "He matches us," Hahn-spirit said. "He's coming alongside. I'm cutting forward again to your time. Hold on!"

The crystal clenched tightly in his hand, Sky-fire-trail obeyed, until at last the ship slowed. Back home, judging by the boxes, and in late evening.

"Quick," Hahn said. "I'm dropping you off. See this?" He held up a small red stick. "It's a marker flare. I set them out there just before you woke up to light you back to the bank. Follow them and you'll be safe. Good-bye, young brave, good luck!"

The next minute, Sky-fire-trail found himself standing on an empty marsh. It was growing dark, but he could just see the time crystal nestling in his palm. He looked about. How long before Hahn-spirit discovered the loss? He must get away, as fast as possible, find somewhere to hide.

At his feet a glowing red stick poked up out of the mud. Hahn-spirit's first marker. The wind gusted, nipping his ears, chilling his shaven scalp. He reached up, encountered his band-of-many-tongues. Sky-fire-trail frowned. He hadn't meant to keep that. An oversight on Hahn-spirit's part, surely—and the god-blanket too! Well, too late to return them now. He pulled the silver stuff about him, stuff light as cobweb, warmer than any skin of deer, then picked his way between markers under the wide and darkening sky; dodging from island to island, slipping, sinking to his knees in icy blackness.

To have seen this place many moons from now, his world vanished without a trace! The grass gone, and the trees, to those monstrous stone towers rearing up to block the sun's light! He recoiled from the memory of massed bodies swarming like termites, the yellow beast crashing through them with terrifying sound.

Sky-fire-trail stopped, remembering Tallspear's lookout, waiting by the bushes, not too far ahead. He drew his god-blanket more tightly about him. He must not bring down Hahn-spirit's wrath on the others. Therefore, he would wait here, on this spot, for Hahn-spirit to come to him, for come he surely would. He pictured Hahn-spirit, standing before the wall of many shining stones, furious, plotting what to do.

Sky-fire-trail's body began to tingle, and there was a faint crackling in his ears. And on his palm, the time stone had begun to spark!

How do you work the magic?

I hold it, so . . . picture where I'm going.

Sky-fire-trail's thought had begun to work that very magic, now! He had begun to take himself back into Hahn-spirit's presence! He cleared his mind of Hahn-spirit, and the ship; staring fixedly at the land all around him.

Sounds carried over the misty air through the gathering darkness. Of heavy feet squelching over the wet ground. As Sky-fire-trail turned, Hahn's great shape lumbered out of the murk. "Young brave! Young brave—wait!"

"Stop the calamity, and you'll get back your stone!"

"I can't! Wait, let me explain!"

Hahn-spirit was coming fast. Too fast. Sky-fire-trail needed a place, the farthest he could go, where he could stop, get his breath, and think what next to do. He remembered the tall, shining cliffs Hahn-spirit had shown him, and as he did so, the stone began to spark, and his skin, to tingle. But at the thought of the teeming crowds, his mind again recoiled, and the swamp began to reappear. Dark, he wanted, and solitude. Trees, rocks, a place to hide. If one small oasis remained in all that madness, this stone would find it out.

Even as he began to picture the place, the stone sparked, and the marsh began to fade.

"No! Sky-fire-trail—no!" Hahn-spirit grabbed for him.

But Sky-fire-trail had already disappeared.

The instant Hahn shouted, he knew his mistake. Too late now. The boy had disappeared. He must return to the ship. A purple crystal in his hand, a space stone only, got him back at once.

The young rascal!

Where had he gone? Only to a place—time—he knew or could picture clearly. His own, of course. But the boy was smart. He could well have fled to either of the two zones he'd visited to witness the calamity. Hahn would have to scan each in turn for the stone's frequency.

First, he tried the boy's own present time, the huddled shelters under the night sky, alert for the slightest signal.

Nothing.

Hahn jumped the ship forward to the first zone he'd taken the boy, the time of the first American President, George Washington—his inaugural year, in fact. Years streamed by in a blur. Nearing his destination, Hahn slowed . . . 1694, 1701 . . . 1745 . . . and skidded to a stop: 1789.

He adjusted the ship's controls to the very instant when

they had materialized with the time stone. There was the sunshine, the boys playing their noisy game. Hahn hovered, careful not to materialize the ship in the middle of that space, scanning the bushes where he'd stood with Sky-fire-trail.

Nothing.

Hahn sighed. Sky-fire-trail was so smart, he might well have shifted through space as well as time. In that case, Hahn would have to scan the whole area. Methodically, he searched the cobbled streets and open tracts for the stone's presence. That young man had been so quick! Foolish, to call out like that. He must be ready next time!

The scan was complete. The boy was not in 1789.

Which left the third time zone, the day on which Hahn had crashed through into Earth's atmosphere. Surely Sky-fire-trail had not gone there? Reason said no. The boy had hated it. Yet the youth was also a hunter, with all the hunter's cunning. Hahn jumped the ship forward, and reaching the date, began his scan for the time stone.

Nothing.

Hahn frowned. Sky-fire-trail had to be here. He hadn't been in his own time or 1789. Of course, they could be chasing around in circles. . . . The boy was quick—what if he'd been too quick? Overshot himself a bit? If so, Hahn told himself, the search could take long—too long, maybe!

Where to start? Well, since Hahn was already there, he decided to scan the zone he was in; backward for a week, then forward. He started back. Days and nights slid by.

Nothing.

Hahn ran the ship forward again, past his date of entry, then on, Saturday, Sunday . . . Tuesday . . . Thursday . . .

Nothing. He'd give it one, two days more, he decided, then hop back to the boy's own time and go around again. He advanced to the Friday, one week on from his arrival.

Still nothing from the sensors, but Hahn had the strangest feeling—*another* feeling! A suspicion that he was getting close. Wait! Hahn paused, his fingers over the controls. *What was happening to him?* Surely he must be malfunctioning? He was not supposed to act on feeling or instinct; indeed, until now he would have said he had none. Always he had acted on what the people of this towered island called logic, or deduction, and on that alone. But from the moment he'd set eyes on this world, the disturbing changes that had been gradually coming over him seemed to be rapidly intensifying. Back in the ship, when Sky-fire-trail had expressed anger, and outrage, and the passionate desire to save his people, Hahn had begun to feel that way himself. And it had hurt, to deny the boy help.

And now? This other kind of feeling, this premonition, this . . . Hahn consulted his built-in thesaurus—*hunch*—that Sky-fire-trail was close was growing too strong to be denied. Hahn slid forward slowly, past midnight, and into the early hours of Saturday: three o'clock, four o'clock, five, five-thirty. Five forty-seven.

Lights flashed, alarms sounded as the ship's sensors caught the time stone's signal. He'd been right! That instinct, that unfounded suspicion had proved correct: the boy was here, now! But not, Hahn saw, checking his elation, in the spot Hahn had taken him. Of course not. Sky-fire-trail had hated the noise, and the crowds. So where then? Where would he have taken himself? Among trees, likely, if there were any.

Hahn collected himself, scanned east and west, working his way systematically northward over windswept, empty streets, grunting in satisfaction as the sensor signal rose in speed and pitch. Getting closer.

Up, up he scanned, across the long wide avenues, up and up, until, as they hit an open stretch, the sensors scored a hit.

Central Park, the data said.

Now Hahn must leave the ship, go out on foot with the space stone. But where to park the pod? He didn't want to materialize it in the middle of one of those huge buildings. He moved the 'scope around the spot on Broad Street where he was hovering, and found a deep excavation site a few blocks to the south. Hahn gazed intently at the monitors in turn, eyeing the shored up earthworks, then nodded. Yes, the ship could transmat that short way. And it should be safe there for a while. The deeply dug foundation was screened from the street above by high wooden walls, and, for the time being anyway, appeared deserted. He transmatted, materialized the ship. Then, taking up the purple space stone, he focused on Sky-fire-trail's exact coordinates, and closed his eyes.

. . .

Frankie awoke on her side, her knees almost to her chin. For a moment she lay still, wondering where she was. Then she remembered, prompted by the dry, metallic taste in her mouth, the tickle in her throat, as there always was when she stayed in motels and breathed their canned and carpeted air. She licked her lips, opened her eyes, raised her head and looked around the room.

It was no longer dark, as it had seemed when she'd gone

to sleep. A crack of light through the bathroom door shone out across brown hotel carpet, brown hotel furniture, cream walls. Over the pastel print of Manhattan Bridge, over her last night's clothes slung across the easy chair under the blinded window, over her mother sleeping in the next bed.

This sort of air always gave Frankie a sick head that nothing could shake. Great, if she got one of those, a really bad one, to rain on Mom's parade. She slid out her hand and picked up her watch off the night table. Five-thirty A.M. Hours to lie and wait before Mom woke up. She lowered herself onto her pillows, and waited. Sure enough, the headache began to get worse. She turned this way, then that. If she didn't do something soon, it would really take hold. Frankie slid from under her covers, picked up her clothes, and crept into the bathroom. Her face looked yellow in the fluorescent light, and her eyes, baggy and horrible. Fresh air, that was what she needed—and quick.

A few moments later, she emerged from the bathroom fully dressed in red sweater and favorite jeans, and navy jacket with the warm plaid lining.

From her sports bag beside her bed, Frankie retrieved her wallet and put it in her right jacket pocket. Never know but she might find a hot chocolate somewhere close. Mom would have a fit if she ever found out, being such a worrywart, but Mom had a built-in weekend sleep-late button and Frankie would be back well before she came to. Frankie straightened slowly, tiptoed across to the door, opened it a sliver, and slipped through.

A few moments later, Frankie stepped from the elevator, zippering up her jacket. Five fifty-four A.M., her watch said.

She turned and walked firmly through the lobby toward the street doors.

She felt the night porter's eye on her as she passed his desk, for one minute thought that he would call her back. She kept right on, her head up, her eyes firmly ahead, and pushed her way unchallenged through the swing doors onto Seventh Avenue.

It was light, just.

Frankie stood for a moment, her hands deep in her pockets, drawing fresh, cold air into her lungs. She looked up and down the avenue, deciding what to do. The city was a dangerous place, Mom never tired of telling her so. But the street looked clear and peaceful enough, and wasn't this a respectable area?

She struck out north to Fifty-ninth Street, crossing over to Central Park South, and stood a moment, taking her bearings. To the west—on her left, was Columbus Circle and the Gulf and Western Building. Way to the east, on her right, lay Fifth Avenue. Her back to the expensive apartments and swish hotels across the road, Frankie leaned over the park wall and breathed in deep. Not much to see; it was too misty. But the air felt good in her lungs, well, better than the hotel air, anyway. Mom had been right about her. Frankie couldn't stand tall buildings too long; she needed trees, and open spaces, and houses people-sized. She walked on eastward, slapping her sneakered feet on the sidewalk, flapping her arms across her chest, breathing deep. For some reason, the clean smell of earth and mist and rotted leaves from over the low stone wall put her in mind of her imaginary brave. ''How's this, O Great One,'' she muttered. She pictured him folding his arms over his fringed leather tunic, looking down his nose, disdaining to answer. "Think you're hot stuff?" she jeered. "Try a brisk trot along Central Park South at six in the morning!"

Snob that he was, he spun on a moccasined heel and took off into the mist.

Show-off!

Frankie looked around curiously. Manhattan was a ghost city at this hour. Save for her, the sidewalk was deserted. Easy to imagine that all the thousands of sleeping people behind those high walls had been spirited away during the night by some alien teleport beam. To her relief, a yellow cab drove by headed for Columbus Circle, and a pasty face peered out the back window. She watched it go, wondering where anybody could be going so early on a Saturday morning, then realized that the cab rider might be thinking the same of her.

The cab, reaching Columbus Circle, turned right toward Broadway, and disappeared, leaving the street deserted once more.

Weird, how now the area was clear, she thought, crossing Sixth Avenue and striding on toward Fifth, you could see the rise and fall of the land under the pavement. The times she'd walked these streets with Mom and never noticed that they went uphill or down. She tried to erase the buildings and the street, and bring back the woodland of long ago . . .

Cold wind blew in Frankie's face, snatching her breath, breaking her reverie. She turned with a slight shudder back toward Seventh Avenue, thinking of the warm hotel.

But her mind, caught up in her new idea, wouldn't quit. Near the Sixth Avenue traffic light, where the pavement curved off into the Park, Frankie halted, staring into the trees, picturing herself alone in primeval forest full of deer and . . . did they have bears on Manhattan in the ancient times? She imagined herself padding through the gloom in deerskin moccasins, unseen, unheard; the perfect hunter, real cool, like—like her imaginary Indian brave, stalking his evening meal. . . .

Mist swirled out from the park, over the wall and onto the sidewalk, blocking the view ahead. She paused again, the bitter cold momentarily forgotten. What if the mist swallowed her, on that deserted morning, and she was swept into that far back time, never to return? She could picture it now; Mom wringing her hands, the banner headlines:

VALLEY STREAM HIGH SCHOOL GIRL
WALKS OUT ONTO SEVENTH AVENUE
AND VANISHES

She had heard tales of things like that happening, of people going through revolving doors and never coming out the other side. She was about to move on, when the mist parted, and something, a blur of movement, startled her, held her in midturn. She gazed off into bushes and mist, frowning. What was it that had caught her eye?

A moment later, she exclaimed in surprise.

Above the mist, the crest of a rocky outcropping floated like a great gray stone canoe. And at its prow, stark against the pearly morning light, stood her imaginary Indian brave—this time, for real!

He was standing still, looking down at her, like a park statue done up in Mohawk hairstyle, beaded headband, a mylar blanket slung over one shoulder.

Beaded? *Mylar?*

Frankie blinked, and looked again.

The guy was gone!

But she'd seen him, she'd swear. Right up on top of that rock. He couldn't have vanished so fast. She swung her legs over the park wall, and scrambled down the bank and up the base of the spur. It was, she found, loaded with toeholds: an easy climb. At the top, she paused where the boy had stood, peering out into mist. She couldn't see a thing. Fifty-ninth Street, only yards off, might have melted clean away. She moved cautiously along the ridge until she reached a small gap severing the rocky spine.

Frankie stood on the edge of the gap, looking across to the spine's continuation the other side. He'd been wearing a beaded headband, and hadn't Webb said there were no beads in Precontact times? And a mylar blanket, for heaven's sake! Agh. The guy was likely a punk from the Village, freaked out on acid or worse. She peered across into the mist. What if he were at that very moment *coming for her?*

She tried to pull herself together. Wasn't she a brown belt? A match for any kid of fourteen, fifteen. Agh. She turned away. She was being dramatic as usual, as Mom called it—and he'd stood straight and tall, not like any bum.

Still. She ought to get down and out of there, fast.

Frankie was swinging her legs over the edge of the spur, when the mist swirled out, and parted, revealing the boy, teetering on the edge of the far spine. He'd been running, hard.

Running from what?

A figure loomed out of the mist behind him; a huge, dark

shape, whose arms were going up to seize him from behind.

"Hey!" she pointed. "Look out!"

The boy whirled, and, she couldn't be sure, but something seemed to flash in his hand. His whole shape began to darken, then it went shadowy, melting into the mist. A moment later, he had disappeared.

For one stunned instant Frankie stood, staring at the huge man left alone on the far rock. The size of him!

"Frankie: what are our three options in karate?"

"Evasion, control, immobilization . . ."

"Meaning?"

"If someone hits, don't be there . . ."

Frankie leapt from the ridge and tumbled pell-mell. Near the bottom of the incline, she catapulted herself down and rolled. Regaining her feet, she started up the opposite bank toward the Fifty-ninth Street wall. Behind her, heavy feet followed, gaining fast. She climbed up a way, slipped back, then scrambled on, the toes of her sneakers skidding on slickery muck: her throat hurt, and she couldn't get enough air going in her chest.

Almost there. She dared not look back.

Frankie reached the wall, was about to vault over, when large hands seized her shoulders from behind and held her fast.

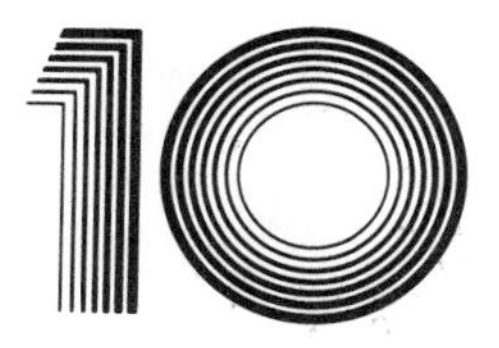

Here, hold up.'' A gentle voice; concerned, and faintly . . . foreign? Strong hands steadied her. ''Are you hurt? Did you scrape yourself?''

Frankie looked up. The eyes, shadowed against the early morning light, looked huge and round, and the face gleamed pale. She took in the strong, well-shaped skull, the short, bristly hair, then moved her gaze to the hand still on her shoulder. The hand fell away.

''You dropped this.'' The other hand came up, holding out her wallet.

Some mugger! Frankie pointed back. ''That boy—did you see how he—''

''Never mind him,'' the man said hurriedly. ''This is not a good place—or time—for a young woman to be out alone. What were you doing?''

The eyes were blue, Frankie observed now. The largest, bluest eyes she'd ever seen. ''I—I had a headache starting, so I came out for some fresh air, only a block or so from my hotel. And I cut in here after that kid.'' Frankie pulled herself up short, not hearing the man's cry of dismay. What was she doing, defending herself to this stranger? Talking to him at all? She looked at him defiantly. "Why did you creep up on him like that?"

The man pushed the wallet at her. "I suggest you put this somewhere before you lose it again," he said, just as Mom would have, and yet the way he said it didn't sound the same at all.

Frankie carefully stuffed the wallet in an inside pocket, and rezippered her jacket, aware of his keen gaze.

"What will you do now?" he asked, as she straightened.

"What'll I do?" Frankie eyed him some more; the navy jumpsuit, bright red sleeves, and running shoes. A uniform, maybe? Did he belong to some kind of institution? Well, he seemed friendly. He hadn't tried to harm her at all, and he'd sure had chance enough. "Go back to the hotel, I suppose." She gripped the wall behind her, ready to climb back onto the avenue. "Well, thanks for the wallet. Good-bye."

"Wait!" the man cried, as Frankie swung a leg. "Before you go, give me your future coordinates—please!"

"My *what?*"

"The name of the place where you're going. Your . . . hotel, did you say? You must," he urged, when Frankie hesitated. "I may need to find you again."

Frankie frowned. "Whatever for?"

"To make sure there's been no harm."

"I said I'm fine," Frankie said loudly. She held out her hands, palms up. "Look: no scratch, no scrape. Okay?"

''Not enough, young woman. That's not the kind of hurt I'm thinking of.''

''No? What other sort is there?'' Frankie swung her other leg.

''Please.'' The man glanced back toward the rock. ''Trust me. Look, I have done you no harm. And I returned your wallet, no? Perhaps if I were to introduce myself,'' he pressed on, as Frankie still did not relent. ''You people do place great value on that, I believe. Here: I'm Hahn. Hahn Ixpodsix.'' He held out his hand.

Frankie swung one leg back again. *Ixpodsix.* Sounded Greek. Still straddling the wall, she leaned over, took the hand, and shook it guardedly. ''Francesca Petersen. Frankie. Who's the guy you're chasing?''

''I call him Sky-fire-trail. Now, please, your coord—''

''Sky-fire-trail!'' What a stunning name! It did sound Indian. She pictured him up on the rock, her imaginary Indian brave for real; taking off like Superman, speeding through the cosmos like a fiery comet, his mylar blanket trailing sparks for thousands of miles. From the Village, she'd bet. She remembered the brightness in his hand, the neat way he'd disappeared. ''What's with you two?''

The blue eyes flickered. ''He has something of mine. I want it back.''

''Then why didn't you stick with him instead of coming after me?''

''Because . . .'' The man frowned, creasing the smoothness of his brow. ''Because you also now have interacted with me. And with Sky-fire-trail.''

"What do you mean, 'interacted'?"

"Surely that's the right word? You, how shall I say, crossed paths with me, and with Sky-fire-trail; that is, we all three met together—*collided*—at a single point in space and time."

"That's no big deal. I mean, people are always bumping into one another. It's certainly nothing to get so upset about."

"Oh, but it is, I assure you."

"You're kidding."

"Frankie, because you saw Sky-fire-trail, you deviated from your proper path in the local space/time continuum, and that—"

"Deviated? From my path in the *what?*"

"Young woman, this is no laughing matter," Hahn said severely. "Had you not seen him, you simply would have gone straight back to your hotel. Instead, you came in here, and also dropped your wallet." He looked back over his shoulder, muttering. "So many changes. Who knows where they all may lead?" He swung back to her decisively. "When I've put things right with Sky-fire-trail, then I'll likely have to deal with you."

Deal with her? Frankie stiffened. "What do you mean?"

"I can't say, yet. Look on the bright side: maybe no harm will come at all, though the ISPYC code says otherwise. I wonder . . ." He closed his eyes and put his head to one side as though listening.

Listening to what? Frankie asked herself, intrigued.

Deviate . . . space/time continuum . . . ipspick—or something like that. Was all this stuff running around in his head? Whatever, he seemed to have quite forgotten her. In fact, thought Frankie, she could take off right now, and he likely wouldn't even notice. But she made no effort to leave. From her perch astride the park wall, she studied the smooth, peaceful face, the eyes closed in, what? He reminded her of karate class, when they all sat for a few minutes in silence at the close of the evening's sessions. But this was some weird spot to pick to meditate. Frankie cleared her throat. "You'll lose that kid, you know."

"Can't be helped." The blue eyes opened wide. "Don't worry, the moment we part, I'll be on his tail again."

"How? However will you find him now?"

"I know where to look."

Frankie recalled how fast the boy had split: there one moment, gone the next. "Sky-fire-trail sure vanished fast," she remarked. "I mean, he just seemed to melt away, and I could swear you had him by the shoulder—"

"Could you now?" he said. "Well, you could be mistak—" Hahn stopped, looking past her.

Frankie twisted around—and cried out. Right beside her, on the avenue side of the park wall, a man stood poised, looking down at them: a giant of a man—close-cropped head, blue eyes; dark blue jumpsuit with bright red sleeves—Hahn's double!

As Frankie sat, transfixed, the twin twisted a fist, pointed the index finger toward them.

"Hold tight, Frankie!" Hahn cried. Before she knew it, he had grabbed her hand and was yanking her down off the wall. Caught off balance, she tumbled into him, bumping her ribs, and the next instant her head began to spin, faster, faster, until he, the park, the twin, everything, dissolved in a whirl of multicolored sparks.

Frankie came to lying in the dark. She tried to raise her head, lowered it again. It felt fuzzy, strange, putting her in mind of a time years ago when she'd passed out after a disastrous Coney Island roller coaster ride. Dry, dusty air caught her throat and her eyes began to water. Her mind clearing some, Frankie recalled her morning walk. The punk kid in Central Park. The stranger, Hahn.

And Hahn's twin.

Frankie swallowed, fighting an urge to cough. She was lying on bare wooden boards lit by a sliver of daylight coming from under a distant door, fading in toward her. Her eyes adjusting, darkness lightened into gloom, revealing long racks of plastic-shrouded dresses stretching away down.

"Frankie?" The whisper made her jump. She struggled up to find Hahn standing behind her. "Frankie, I am so sorry. The trouble before was nothing compared to this."

"Hahn, where are we? How did we get here? *What's going on?*"

"Hush." Hahn looked around. "I cannot name where we are. I picked the spot at random. I'm afraid you'll have to make your own way from now on, Frankie. See that door? Go, now. Quickly, while you can!"

Even before he finished speaking, the air beside him filled with shadow, and the shape of the twin began to form.

"*Run!*" Hahn cried.

Frankie ran. At the door, there came another shout—Hahn's? Then she was through, and out.

She found herself in a dark and dirty loading bay. On the door, a battered sign said "Lewis's Seventh Avenue Fashions, Inc. Trucks only." A garment factory warehouse, Frankie realized; deserted, of course, on this early Saturday morning. She stood, getting her bearings, pulling her thoughts together. If this was the garment district, she must be somewhere between Thirtieth and Fortieth streets. But she couldn't recall how she had gotten there from Central Park South. Only that she must have been unconscious. For how long? Frankie glanced at her watch. Only six fifty-two! How could Hahn have gotten them so far south in that short time! She frowned. Something strange was going on here, *really* strange, she told herself, recalling now the way Hahn's twin had started to come out of thin air.

She thought of the two men back inside the warehouse. Brothers, like Cain and Abel . . .

Run, Hahn had told her. And so she should. They obviously had a feud going, and none of her business. She ought to go now, as Hahn had bidden her, back to the hotel. Mom wouldn't begin to awaken until nine at least, but even so. Frankie emerged from the shadow of the bay onto the narrow sidewalk, then looked back. Whatever was going down, Hahn was in trouble, deep trouble. She felt the bulk of her wallet inside her jacket, recalled the concern in the man's blue eyes. Concern for her. . . . *to be sure there's been no harm . . .*

Hahn had paused there on her account. On her account,

he'd missed catching Sky-fire-trail. And in returning her wallet, he'd stayed behind. She thought back to Hahn's strange words: *So many changes. Who knows where they all may lead?* Although she herself couldn't understand his meaning, she was beginning to suspect he knew what he was talking about. Look at the mess Hahn is in already, she thought guiltily. Oh, she couldn't, wouldn't ditch him now. But what to do? Frankie glanced along the narrow street. A group of men stood at the corner, smoking. She hurried toward them partway, thinking to ask them for help, then faltered. What could she say? There are two hulks—identical hulks—in that garment warehouse, and I think there's going to be a terrible fight. How come they're in there? I don't know, but I just saw one of them appearing right out of thin air . . .

With a quick shake of her head, Frankie ran back to the warehouse, and slipped inside.

Silence.

Where were they, Hahn and his brother?

A blue flash lit the rafters. Frankie groped her way in, trailing her fingers for guidance along the rows of plastic bags, then stopped.

Just ahead, the twins stood facing each other, blocking the aisle. The instant she saw them, more light burst between them. The nearer one went down, and, as he fell, there came another flash. The downed twin rolled; the other raised a red-clad arm to fire again. "Lasers," Frankie whispered.

Which one was Hahn? No time to find out!

"*Ki*-hap!" With a ferocious yell, Frankie grabbed a clothes rack and sent it rolling down the aisle.

The standing figure looked toward her, startled at the outburst, and, as he did so, light flashed from the floor. The upright twin dropped his firing arm, staggered, and began to fall. But before he hit the floor, his shape faded, then disappeared.

The fallen twin was lying back again, quite still.

Hahn—or the brother?

Frankie crept forward, and crouched. The eyes were closed, and . . . She wrinkled up her nose, sniffing. There was a faint odor in the air, of scorched cloth, and . . . *antiseptic?* She leaned closer. There, above the heart—a hole was burned in the dark blue cloth of the jumpsuit—but no sign of blood or wound! Frankie put a hand to the neck, feeling for a pulse.

At her touch, the blue eyes opened, starting her up onto her feet. She stood poised, ready to flee, but then the eyes focussed and the smooth features twisted with concern. "Frankie."

Frankie puffed out in relief. "Your brother split, just like Sky-fire-trail. You scored, I'd say." And thought, with what? There was no sign of weapon lying around. She glanced to the scorch hole above his heart. "But he hit you worse. You okay?"

"I will be," he said. He tried to sit, but fell back with a groan.

"Here, let me." Frankie crouched again, slipped her hands under his arms, and tried to haul him up. "Come on," she urged. "You've got to move."

He came up a way, then flopped back again. "I can't," he murmured, and Frankie caught the word *disrupted.*

''Hahn? Hahn!'' No reply. She leapt up in alarm. ''I'll fetch help.''

''No! Go—please . . .'' His voice trailed off, his eyes closed.

''Hahn!'' Frankie got back down, seized his wrist. Nothing. No pulse in the neck, either. She laid her head on his chest, listening for a heartbeat. Still nothing. Was he breathing? Should she try mouth-to-mouth? She was just checking when there came a thump on the door and a murmur of voices.

Hahn moved, jumping her out of her skin. ''Frankie—'' He seemed to be trying to reach a pocket in his jumpsuit leggings.

''What is it, Hahn?'' She put her ear close to his lips. ''Hahn?''

''Stone,'' he whispered, eyes still closed. Frankie raised the pocket flap, and reaching inside, felt the rough edges of a crystal. She drew it out. Hard to tell in the light but it might be an amethyst. As she set the stone on his palm and closed his fingers about it, the outside door crashed open and heavy feet stampeded into the room.

''Hey, you—on your feet!''

Shapes lumbered toward her against the light. Frankie froze, her hand still clasped over Hahn's. In that instant, a tingling started up her arm and spread through her body. The air around her shimmered, blurring a cop's dark bulk. Her head was spinning again, just as in Central Park, only this time she didn't pass out because she calmly shut her eyes while the air cracked and spat like an old cable shorting out. She still seemed to be kneeling, holding Hahn's hand closed about the stone, yet she had a sense of *traveling,* of wind streaming past.

The noises stopped, the wind died. Wherever, she and Hahn had arrived.

Frankie opened her eyes.

She *was* still kneeling over Hahn, but the warehouse had disappeared. They were now in an oval chamber sheathed in polished silver alloy studded with banks of tiny control lights winking out of sync.

Frankie leaned over on all fours, feeling giddy again, while Hahn lay still as death. As soon as she could, she bent and listened to his chest, heard nothing. She huddled closer to him. He was breathing. That was as far as her CPR training went. At a loss now, she looked around.

In the middle of the floor beside them lay a large cylinder, like a huge broad bean shell. To one end of the oval cabin, a flat wall glowed with rows of lighted TV screens—except that—Frankie stepped closer—the pictures were in 3-D! Holographs? Each showing a wide expanse of churned up earthwork from a different viewpoint. Tiny scale models, like the ones in the museum, only these looked for real.

Frankie thought back to the dark factory, to the image of Hahn's brother dissolving, the way Sky-fire-trail had. The way she and Hahn must have done, going from Central Park to the garment factory, and thence on to this place.

Teleportation? As in "Star Trek" and "Blake's 7"?

She looked around the shiny, silver cabin, realized she was trembling. "Hahn—hey, Hahn!" She shook his arm. No response. She should get help, but how? There was not a door or window anywhere. Oh, what had she gotten herself into?

''I can't find a way out, sir.''

''Then better not to have gotten in, wouldn't you say?''

''All very well, Mr. Ho,'' she grumbled to herself. ''But it's a bit late to think of that now.''

''Frankie.''

Frankie came to. Hahn's eyes had opened, and he was looking at her. ''Please, you see the LSRM behind you?''

LSRM. Did he mean the cylinder? ''Ye-es.''

''Good. Now see the control panel around the far side?''

Frankie went to look. Yes, halfway along its base. About a foot square, and encrusted in colored stones. ''Uh-huh.''

''Press the green crystal, please.''

She did so, and at once the LSRM lid began to rise on hinges. Inside? A mylar-padded bed. Frankie shifted uneasily. It looked awfully like a coffin. The lid was studded with lights, unlit, and wires protruded from all sides. At the head was a metal cap, attached to the cylinder walls by myriads of tubes and wires intertwined. ''What is the LSRM? Where are we? How did we get here?''

''It's my Life Support and Repair Module—a diagnostic/repair unit. This is my ship. And—'' Hahn reached out, wincing, and tried unsuccessfully to drag himself forward.

Ship? Frankie moved to help him, heaved on the solid weight of him, edged him inch by painful inch toward the LSRM's smooth side. *''Ship?''*

Grunting with the effort, Hahn gripped the edge of the LSRM and tried once more to pull himself upright.

Frankie pumped herself up with a couple of good deep breaths as Mr. Ho had taught her, then, hooking her hands under Hahn's arms, she hoisted him until he was high enough to topple over the edge and lie flat on the silver cushions, looking up at her. She backed off, fighting thoughts of friendly Draculas and space-age crypts.

Again, Hahn homed in with uncanny accuracy. "I am a friend, Frankie. I would never harm you. And I certainly didn't intend for you to come here—though if you hadn't . . ." He sounded exhausted. "Frankie"—she could scarcely hear him now—"fit the cap to my head."

Frankie poked the cap gingerly. Nothing happened. Encouraged, she took firm hold with both hands and fitted it to Hahn's scalp. The moment it was on, Hahn sighed in relief. "Now press the purple, the yellow, the violet, then the orange crystal, in that order, Frankie, please."

She moved to comply. *Purple . . . yellow . . . violet . . . orange.* "Okay?"

"Okay. Now the green one again . . ."

Slowly, the lid came down, until it had shut tight on Hahn's face. In the movies, the organ would be rising to a crescendo, toccata and fugue in something minor. . . . From the LSRM base came a quiet hum. Frankie walked all around it. No sign of any ventilation.

"Hahn?" He was going to suffocate. Should she raise the lid again? The controls began to wink rapidly, all at different rates. What was going on inside? Frankie straightened up thoughtfully. Diagnostic/repair unit, Hahn had called it. Sounded like something in a garage.

It must be healing him. How long would it take?

Well, however long, Frankie thought, she was here for the duration, so she might as well begin to practice what she had been taught and set about pulling herself together. Hitching up her jeans, Frankie hunkered down beside the LSRM, where she crossed her legs, set her hands firmly on her knees, and closed her eyes.

"Thanks, Frankie." Frankie started at a light touch on her shoulder.

Hahn was standing beside her, looking perfectly recovered. She herself was lying slumped against the side of the cylinder. Had she dozed off? Must've, she thought, scrambling to her feet. "In the warehouse your heart had stopped beating. I thought you were dead."

Hahn shook his head. "It hadn't."

"But I checked."

"Frankie," Hahn tapped his chest, "there's nothing in here *to* beat." He smiled. "Are you hungry? You Earthlings need recharging often, as I understand it."

"Nothing—to beat?"

"My heart's a solid-state power pack. I'm not human, you see. What food do you like?"

Frankie stared openmouthed. "Not human?"

"You're scared?"

Scared? She was paralyzed! Had she finally flipped? Was she on some kind of space-age Alice in Wonderland kick?

She'd dreamed up an Indian brave, and that guy Sky-fire-trail had popped out of the blue, large as life. She'd dreamed about a "mind child," and here was Hahn, inside an egg! Pure, 100 percent, hi-tech Lewis Carroll, serve her right! "Don't tell me," she said, sarcastically. "You're an artificial intelligence in a human body: a twenty-six million dollar man."

"Close. Look, say what food you like and we'll talk, okay?"

He was being like Mom again, thought Frankie. But she really was hungry, come to think. "Pizza," she said, glancing around for the galley.

"Pizza." Hahn closed his eyes briefly, in the way that he had. "Can do. How would you like it?" he said, opening them again.

"Sicilian style—well done, with extra mushrooms. And a vanilla shake."

"Sounds . . . interesting. I think I'll try some with you." Hahn set the LSRM sliding into the floor, then went over to a sort of fancy locker wall with control panels beside each door. He tapped out a rapid code on one of these panels and almost immediately a door pinged open, revealing a white plastic tray with white plastic dishes and mugs. Some microwave!

"Here we are." Hahn set the tray down on the spot where the LSRM had been, sat himself crosslegged, and gestured Frankie to follow.

Frankie slowly sat, her eyes on the tray.

An important part of preparing any meal, as Mrs. Sterne, Home Ec. class, had made her write down, was the presentation. Not only must the food be tasty, it must also look and smell tasty, stimulating the appetites of those who are about to partake of it. As she said *pizza,* Frankie's mouth had begun to water at the thought of bubbles of melted mozzarella, the tang of tomato sauce, luscious mushrooms piled on top, and hot, crispy pastry crust all around. At the ping, she could almost smell the oregano.

It was with a certain amount of disappointment, therefore, that she eyed the bowls, the aroma of fresh-baked pizza giving place to fancied whiffs of bug killer. In them lay what looked like slug pellets.

Hahn put one in his mouth. "Ow," he warned. "Careful not to burn yourself."

Frankie picked up a pellet, examined it dubiously, placed it on her tongue. For a moment it lay there like dry nothing, then suddenly it swelled up and grew warm, then hot, and she was chewing on the most delicious fresh Sicilian pizza she'd ever tasted. She washed it down with a long swallow of thick, rich vanilla shake, ice-cold—and real. As was this place, and Hahn, no less. "A mind child, for sure; in a real, live human body," she murmured.

"I beg your pardon?"

"Oh, nothing," Frankie said. "I was just talking to myself. I do it a lot to fill the quiet."

"Me, too," Hahn said.

"Oh? You wouldn't happen to daydream too?"

"Daydream? What is that?"

"Never mind." Frankie looked around. A ship, Hahn had called it. But what kind of ship? She looked at Hahn incredulously. "Don't tell me: you're not only a mind child, but a star child, as well. An alien, and this"—she waved her arm about—"is your spaceship!"

"Right on both counts." Hahn smiled, a little wryly, it seemed to Frankie. "I'm what the folk on my world call a *bio-tech:* part flesh, part this." He flapped his hands at the crystals working all around them. "I wasn't born, but made in a lab. My living, 'bio' parts, were grown in tanks. My 'tech' parts were embedded into my tissues as they grew: wires thinner than hairs into my bones and nerves, crystals into the cells of my brain. Hence my name."

"Your *name?* 'Hahn'?"

He nodded. "It's an acronym: H.A.H.N., standing for Humanoid Android for Hyperspace Navigation. I'm really just a remote extension of the ship."

"Oh, no." Frankie shook her head emphatically. "No, you're not. You're not a 'just' anything. And certainly no android. You're a man, Hahn. A cyborg, maybe, but very much a man for all that."

Hahn looked puzzled. "Cyborg?"

" 'Droids are 100 percent mechanical. A cyborg is part machine, but made of living human cells—the way you are. On Earth, anyway. Check your data and see."

Hahn closed his eyes. "Why, you're right," he said, opening them again. "You folk make finer distinctions than the people of my world. There, my artificially engineered being, bio or not, is android."

"Why that's appalling!" Frankie cried. "As well as grossly inaccurate. Huh, I'd have thought folk with that level of technology would know better. Don't they respect you at all?''

''Respect me? Oh, yes. I am an android of the highest class.''

''I mean as a person. They gave you a last name, didn't they?''

Ixpodsix.

''That simply indicates that I'm a class nine unit, and my pod—that is, ship—is number six.''

''But that's disgraceful! It's as bad as—as the old days when we used human beings for slaves!'' A miracle mind child incarnate, Frankie thought disgustedly, and his people treat him no better than a vacuum cleaner! ''I went to a show last Sunday,'' she said. ''Here, at the Natural History Museum. They talked about . . . people like you.''

''Oh, really?'' Hahn closed his eyes for a moment, then, with a slight shake of his head, got up and put his finger to a section of the wall. A moment later, nodding, he sat down again, ''Ummm, they're on the right track, but it'll still take a while before they can make someone like me. You see, the trouble is not so much cloning cells or making minds, but interfacing the two. I see you base your technology on silicon.''

''The chips, you mean? Why not?''

''Crystal is better, Frankie.''

''Oh,'' Frankie said. ''Hahn, when you stuck your finger in that wall just now—''

He touched his temple. ''I didn't have it stored in here. So I tapped into the main terminal; scanned the whole show. In binary code. I can scan that size instantaneously. A useful function."

"I bet," Frankie said enviously, thinking of upcoming midterm tests.

"I can not only scan," he went on, "but store—quite a few megabytes before it gets crowded in here." He touched his skull again. "This way, I function quite efficiently, at least, I did until . . ."

"Until what, Hahn?"

His blue eyes looked troubled. "I have started to malfunction in the most disturbing way."

"Oh, Hahn. I'm sorry. What is it? You losing memory, or something?"

Hahn shook his head. "It's worse. You see, although I look like a human, I am programmed only to record, observe, and transmit data. I am absolutely not programmed for emotion." He reached over and gathered their empty dishes onto the tray.

"But that's absurd." Frankie laughed shortly. "You're as human as anybody I've ever met. And more kind and caring than a lot of people I know. So what—oh." Frankie nodded, understanding suddenly. "That's what's bothering you."

"That's it." Hahn carried the tray back to the storage wall, posted it. "Frankie," he turned to face her. "My system is breaking down."

"Breaking down?" Frankie shook her head. "No, Hahn. You have it figured quite wrong. It's not your so-called system breaking down: it's your nature breaking *out!*"

"Go on." Hahn folded his arms and leaned against the wall.

"The way I see it," Frankie went on, "you're basically no less human than I. We're both grown from primary cells, aren't we? The only difference is I was grown inside another human being, while you were grown in a dish."

"But I was *programmed,* Frankie."

"Me, too," she said. "We call it genetics. I'm a mixture of different genes carrying coded messages from each side of my family. Your bio cells carry the same kind of DNA, also, Hahn."

"But with me," Hahn argued, "nothing was left to chance. My primary cells were carefully selected to make me for this job."

"We call that selective breeding. We rear animals for different specialized purposes. And we also have been doing it with humans for thousands of years through arranged marriages, though they're less common now, thank goodness. Whichever way you look at it, Hahn, you're as human as I. I bet you have lots of friends back home."

"Friends? Home?" Hahn shook his head. "This ship is the only home I know. And I've never had friends. In fact, you and Sky-fire-trail are the very first people I have ever had contact with directly."

"No *friends?*" Frankie stared. "Never? Not even when you were young?"

"I never was a child like you. This is how I came. And this is how I stay. This is my default mode, as they call it, selected for optimum efficiency."

"Never a kid?" Frankie couldn't bear it. She thought of her third birthday party, the purple candles Mom had combed the Island for, that being Frankie's favorite color at the time.

And she remembered how she, Frankie, had burned her fingers trying to grasp the flames. She thought of Anna. Anna had been at that party—and they were still buddies. Why, she even remembered their first day together at kindergarten . . . For all the fights and bad times, Frankie couldn't imagine life without Anna and the other kids. She thought how sorry she felt for herself some days, going home to an empty house. How she daydreamed, and talked aloud to fill the quiet. But suppose she were suddenly to lose her memory, to start life from this moment, her past wiped out—that would be lonely for sure. She looked up. "You surely have some compensation. What about hobbies? How do you fill your spare time?"

"Spare time?" Hahn smiled. "I have none."

"But—everybody gets tired. Everybody needs a break."

Hahn shook his head. "I recharge instantly. And if damaged, I simply repair myself. The LSRM can fix anything, from bio cell regeneration to tech part replacement. Unless I am totally destroyed, I shall go on functioning to infinity."

Infinity. Frankie shivered. "And you never felt lonely?"

"Until now. That's the trouble. You see, as I just said, I'm programmed not to feel anything—and come to think, maybe it is as well. This loneliness, for instance: it makes me . . ." Hahn seemed at a loss.

"Sad?"

"I suppose. Fortunately, in between planets, I lie in stasis in the LSRM, until a signal activates me. And that's the way it's been until now."

"Hahn, why do you travel around like this without ever going home? What is your job? Why are you here?"

Hahn threw up his hands in mock defense. "Questions, questions! I'm not supposed to tell."

She laughed shortly. "You think I'm going to blab? I can see it now:

VALLEY STREAM SCHOOL GIRL SHARED PIZZA
WITH ALIEN IN FLYING EGG!

" 'We ate Sicilian pizza, extra mushrooms, crust well-done,' claims Frankie Petersen. 'Drank vanilla shake, discussed advanced robotics and interplanetary travel.' "

Hahn sighed. "All right." He sat down again. "I'm with ISPYC. It's an intergalactic conservation group—one of many."

Frankie whistled. Like Greenpeace. "What's to conserve?"

"Earth, and quite a few other planets like her."

"Earth? What are you supposed to be saving her from?"

"Maybe nothing, Frankie. But right throughout the galaxies there are planets needing room to expand. Populations—human and otherwise—desperate enough to seize other people's living space."

"You mean they'd try to take our turf?"

Hahn nodded. "There's a run right now on oxygen-bearing worlds. So there's a search on for planets like yours, and ships waiting to bring alien settlers keen to begin a new life."

"But that's terrible!" Frankie cried, alarmed. "No one has the right to take another's land!"

"In theory, maybe. But in practice, it goes differently. Don't judge too harshly, Frankie," Hahn said. "You see, when the need is great, a species will do anything to survive."

"This outfit of yours—ISPYC—where does it come in?"

"It's like this: when what we call global piracy got so bad, the Intergalactic Council passed laws to stop it. But these laws only drove the practice, as you say, under the table. So voluntary organizations formed, like mine, to patrol the star-lanes, to try to keep the global seizures down." He shifted his long legs, recrossed them. "I'm one of many scouts searching the galaxies for prime planets like yours: sitting targets for takeover. Having found you, I report your status as an already settled planet with ISPYC. ISPYC then records Earth's status into the Intergalactic Register, and from that moment she is officially protected from alien encroachment."

"That's all right, then."

"Not really, Frankie. I can't beam the data back until I'm clear of your star system. And as you can see, I'm grounded, maybe for good."

"How do you mean 'grounded'?"

She listened, while Hahn explained who his "brother" was, how Pod #24 H.A.H.N. had come from nowhere and shot him down over Manhattan.

"You were the fireball!"

Hahn nodded. "As I came down, I managed to pull back through time to where there were no buildings or people, only swamp and trees."

"Through *time?*"

"Yes, Frankie."

"Sky-fire-trail—he's a *real* Manhattan Indian?"

"Yes."

Frankie closed her eyes, let out a long, slow whistle. Sky-fire-trail: no punker, but the real genuine Precontact McCoy, like those tiny scale models in the Museum of the American Indian. Last Saturday, when she'd stood by that model village, Hahn had been in that very era! She saw again the tall figure looking down on her, the Mohawk hairdo, the mylar blanket and beaded headband, no doubt gifts from . . . "Oh, heavens! And he's running loose in Central Park right *now!* How did he get there in the first place, Hahn?"

"It's a long story, but my crash caused some disruption; shifts in his local area."

Space/time continuum, Hahn had called it. "What shifts?"

Hahn told her; about the crash coinciding with the boy's birth, and the shaman's prophecy. How he'd taken Sky-fire-trail to the two future time zones, shown him the coming calamity. How Sky-fire-trail had demanded that Hahn rewrite history, how Hahn had had to refuse.

"You mean you could?"

He nodded. "But at who knows what cost? It's against the ISPYC code to meddle with a planet's internal affairs."

"Even a little bit?"

Hahn sighed. "Frankie, you're an intelligent young woman. You know the answer to that."

She sure did. The quarrels she had with Mom over those TV wildlife shows! The way the photographers zoomed in as the lioness took the gazelle.

"But it's obscene! Those guys could stop it! They're right there, on the spot!"

"So what does the lioness take home to her cubs, Frankie?"

"You mean it's okay for the lioness to kill, being a mom. What if the deer's a mommy, too?"

"Be rational, Frankie. That kind of sentimental thinking and misguided interference would seriously upset the ecology and disrupt the natural process of evolution. . . ."

Frankie eyed Hahn stubbornly. "I still don't like it. It's not fair."

Hahn spread his hands. "Me neither, especially now that I have begun to feel. Oh, Frankie, I wish I could help, but the ISPYC code is categorical."

Frankie persisted. "If you came to save all of us—how can you refuse to help one small part?"

"Frankie, Frankie." Hahn wagged a finger. "Your argument is specious. My brief is with extra-terrestrial interference. Sky-fire-trail's plight is due to purely internal factors. Even so, I did try to help. I showed him what lay ahead to save him from wasting his time, from trying to do the impossible—and look at the result. Frankie, Sky-fire-trail's future is history; it's over and done. I was never intended to go back to his day, certainly not to materialize and interact with it." He leaned forward. "And think, young woman, think what it might mean to you and your kind if I did."

"But you—" Frankie stopped.

". . . *no one has the right to take another's land* . . ."

"Oh," she said at last, in a low voice. To restore things, to put things back the way they were in Sky-fire-trail's time, would mean no settlers from over the oceans, no colonies, and so no USA. "I guess in that case I wouldn't be here."

"Exactly."

"And I thought I had troubles," Frankie muttered. "Poor Sky-fire-trail." There must be something she could do.

Hahn climbed to his feet. "Frankie, I'm afraid it's time to go."

"The way I see it," Frankie said hurriedly. "You have three things to deal with. One is your broth—I mean, the other H.A.H.N. Un-Hahn, I think I'll call him. Then there's Sky-fire-trail. And we have to get this ship off the ground. Where do we start?"

Hahn glanced to a red light blinking rapidly high in the wall. "Not we, Frankie. First, I'm putting you off near your hotel. Then I'll go after Sky-fire-trail, and retrieve my time stone."

Time stone! "Is it like the purple one that brought us here?"

"Yes, except the one Sky-fire-trail has can also transmat through time."

Transmat? That meant teleport. Frankie whistled. "He's figured how to use it?"

"He most certainly has."

"There's just the one time stone?"

"The only remote one. There's another, but it's built in." Hahn pointed to a large colorless quartz nugget embedded in the wall.

"Then how do you follow him?"

"I shift through time via the ship. It's clumsy, and dangerous, because there's always the chance of materializing into something. An object this size could cause great damage."

‘‘And then? When you’ve found the right time zone?’’

Hahn sighed. ‘‘Once I locate him, I lock on, and take off on foot with my remote space stone.’’

As he’d done in Central Park. ‘‘How *do* you locate him, in the first place, I mean?’’

‘‘Each crystal gives off a distinctive signal.’’

‘‘You mean, like a homing beacon?’’

‘‘Exactly.’’

‘‘That’s neat—except doesn’t that mean Un-Hahn can find it, too?’’

‘‘Don’t even think it, but yes.’’

‘‘Oh boy. You really do have trouble. And Sky-fire-trail, too. Well, not to panic. Un-Hahn was also hit. So he could still be fixing himself, which gives us time.’’

Hahn shook his head. ‘‘Not *us,* Frankie. I’m sorry, but I really must drop you off now.’’

Frankie made a show of looking at her watch. ‘‘It is eight-oh-four and fifty-five seconds. Mom won’t surface for hours yet,’’ she said crossing her fingers. ‘‘And I’m not leaving in the middle. So like it or no, Hahn, I’m sticking with you.’’

"Frankie, I've already tried to explain," Hahn said.
"Look," she said. "You yourself admitted you were glad I was around." Not fair, reminding him how she'd saved him from Un-Hahn but it was all the clout she had.

"That I did, and I was. I owe you much, young woman. But—"

"No buts, Hahn. I wish, I really wish I could see Skyfire-trail once more. Couldn't I go along, just until you catch him? When you drop him off back in his own time, you can drop me off back here. *Please.*"

"Well, I—"

Hahn was weakening, she could see. "Besides," she said, pressing her advantage, "if Un-Hahn pops again, you're sure to be glad of me." A mistake, she knew it as soon as the words were out.

"Frankie, there is too much danger in it. And we've caused enough disruption already."

"Just suppose," she said quickly, "I hadn't been there in

the warehouse, and Un-Hahn had beaten you down. What would have happened then?''

Hahn appeared to consider. ''Well,'' he said at last. ''Reason tells me that if, as seems certain, he is working against ISPYC now, he would gather up evidence of my visit and delete it.''

''So that no one would ever know you'd been here?''

''That's right.''

''And so then Earth would be unprotected. How awful,'' Frankie said. ''But how would he ditch a thing this size?'' She waved an arm around the ship's cabin. ''You said the drives are damaged, that it can't fly.''

Hahn pointed up. ''See there?''

Standing on tiptoe, Frankie peered at a small panel set flush with the wall. She saw the symbol scratched on its surface, a figure eight lying on its side; and the dark stone behind. ''That's the sign for infinity.''

''Correct.'' Hahn nodded. ''That, Frankie, is my doomsday button, my ticket to a journey of no return.''

''What do you mean?''

''Break that seal and press that stone, and this ship and all in it go on a one-way trip to eternity.''

The words struck Frankie cold. ''But Un-Hahn couldn't do that without sending himself, too.''

''Oh, but he could. There's a ten-second lapse, plenty of time to transmat out. Simple, eh, Frankie? Simple and clean. Then he can freely report to whoever owns him now that there's a world in this sector just waiting for oxygen-loving life forms in need of extra space.''

"But it won't happen," she declared. "You're a match for him."

"You reckon?" Hahn broke into a smile. "Well, let's hope you're right. Anyway, all this makes it the more imperative to get back my time stone. So if you'll just tell me where to drop you—"

"Hahn, *please* let me stay with you. For a while."

"It's against—"

"—ISPYC code." She folded her arms. "Well, as you said, we've already collided, and how. So isn't it a bit late to worry about all that?"

"I suppose." Hahn sighed, blew out his cheeks, exactly like Mom on the verge of giving in. "All right. I let you watch me locate that young brave, then I put you both off, as you said. Agreed?"

"Agreed." Frankie could scarcely hide her elation.

"Well, now, if you're going to help at all . . ." From the locker wall, Hahn produced a headband worked in tiny crystal beads, like the one she'd seen Sky-fire-trail wearing. "One universal translator. Put it on."

Frankie slipped it over her head. It felt cold for a moment, and curiously heavy. She felt a faint ache in her temples, but even as she put a hand to her head, it released and she felt nothing. "You mean this will make me understand *Indian?"* Upper Delaware, according to Webb.

"Broadly speaking."

"Meaning?"

"Frankie, just knowing what other folk call things doesn't tell you how they feel about them."

"For instance?"

"Sky-fire-trail says, 'auke.' You'll hear, 'land,' or 'earth.' But that word has different associations for each of you."

"I don't understand. Dirt is dirt everywhere."

"There you go," Hahn said. "To Sky-fire-trail, earth is not what you think of as 'dirt.' To him it is respected, sacred, even. A source of life and sustenance. It certainly would have great mystical value."

Frankie nodded slowly. She thought she understood. What Hahn was saying would apply to other things, things she couldn't dream of. She wouldn't want to act gross or offensive in front of Sky-fire-trail through her ignorance. "I guess when we meet, I'd better watch it," she said.

Hahn nodded. "Just remember the band's limitations. Now," he went on, going to the monitor wall, "since we're here, we'll scan this time zone. Watch the central box, Frankie."

As she watched, earthworks gave way to a gap between two tall towers on Broad Street. Not very busy on that cold Saturday, but still enough people battled the icy wind along the sidewalks on that late morning.

"That was where you took Sky-fire-trail?"

"The very spot."

"But I saw him in Central Park."

Hahn nodded. "He's obviously found how to get around in the same timeframe. So—let's scan the whole neighborhood."

"And then?"

"Once I locate the stone, I transmat."

We transmat, Frankie amended silently. She watched, while Hahn scanned.

Nothing happened.

"He's not in this time zone at all."

"Not even Central Park?"

"Not even."

Frankie pictured Un-Hahn, repaired and also scanning for signals. "What if Un-Hahn picks up the stone first?"

"Don't!" Hahn looked worried. "Frankie, I'm taking the ship back."

She was going to travel through time! "What will it feel like?"

Hahn kept his eyes on the control wall, pressed crystals in rapid succession. "In the ship, nothing to it. You don't even know you're moving."

She waited. "When do we go?"

"We're here."

"Where?"

Hahn pointed.

Each box showed a rough-paved street lined with brick houses, each from a slightly different angle. Facing them, at the far end of the street was a large, white, gracious building, like a public library, with a pillared portico and tall chimneys.

"Where are we?" It looked vaguely Village.

"Broad Street, 1789, looking toward Federal Hall."

"1789! George Washington's inaugural year!" Frankie looked out at the passersby in fancy costume, realized with a start it was their everyday dress. "Can they see us?" She remembered Hahn saying that he never materialized in local time zones, if he could help it.

"No. We're dematerialized."

Frankie looked at Hahn, then down at herself. They both seemed solid enough, and she felt solid, too. "We are? How do you do that?"

"I'm *random-oscillating* the ship between nanoseconds. We're quite normal in here. But we're hovering outside the local space/time continuum. If you were out there, you'd see nothing of the ship. In fact, you'd walk right through it as though it weren't there."

We're like ghosts, thought Frankie. Or bouncing quarks. She studied the monitors. "I can't see Sky-fire-trail."

"Let's take a closer look. We stood . . . there." Hahn zoomed the 'scope in on a clump of bushes standing back from the sidewalk, halfway down the road.

No sign of him.

Down the road a piece, a bunch of rowdies played tag. Farther along, a girl of about eighteen in a long black dress and white apron and bonnet filled twin pails at a water pump, working the heavy iron handle up and down.

"He's not here, either." Hahn panned the 'scope through the streets, passing carriages, people on horseback, loaded carts, then everything blurred. "Not anywhere in this time zone."

"Where now?"

"Well, we could be chasing around in circles, but there's one more place." This time, the ship lurched slightly, sending Frankie back against the LSRM. By the time she was straightened up, the monitors were dark cavities in the silver wall. Night time. A full moon rode high in a clear night sky, highlighting dense, spiky trees, deep in snow. Beyond the trees were clustered some thirty or so low shelters. They looked familiar. She felt a quick flick of excitement. There—right there, stood a village just like the scale model she'd seen in the Museum of the American Indian!

Hahn switched to full surveillance, filling each box with a view of the settlement from slightly different angles. Frankie gazed intently into each one, fascinated. What wonderful huge trees. And so many of them, ranged around the little village like a protective wall. In the midst of the settlement was a bonfire around which people were gathered, watching something roasting in the flames. The folk were warmly wrapped in hide leggings, and wore blankets and wrappings about their heads, and skins were strapped about their feet. Nevertheless, Frankie shivered to see them standing out there, ankle-deep in the snow.

A yellow crystal flashed, and a bell pinged.

Hahn exclaimed in satisfaction.

"The homing signal, Hahn?"

"Yes. The stone's here. Not by the fire . . ." He swept the 'scope farther into the trees beyond the tipis.

Frankie and Hahn cried out together. "There he is!"

Hahn zoomed in on a bright speck, a hint of silver slipping around behind the outer tipis. He held up the purple stone. "Wait here, Frankie. I'll be there and back before you know it."

"Two are better than one, Hahn. Oh, please! You'll be sorry if you lose him again!" She grabbed his arm as the space stone flashed.

Frankie clung to Hahn as her head whirled and the ship's cabin disappeared. When her head cleared, wind, sharp as a paring knife sheared past her ears. She found herself standing knee deep in crusted snow, the bitter cold already striking through her jeans and sneakers and her warm lined jacket. She let go Hahn's arm, and staggered a step or two, then recovered.

A high moon floated overhead, pale compared with the cozy flames of the bonfire. Layered scents of baking meats and woodsmoke, and the quiet murmur of human voices gusted past on the icy wind.

Frankie gazed about eagerly, remembering the model. What would Bingham Webb say if he knew where she was now! Ahead lay the shelters. Beyond them she could just make out the fish-drying poles, and baskets stacked underneath. Looking down on the model settlement in the museum, she'd felt only how rough, and stark, and bleak it looked. *Depressing*. But from where she stood now she could think only how simply it blended with the land around it. She took a good, deep breath, filling her lungs, savoring the earthy odors and the unmistakable tang of snow. Sky-fire-trail's village, harboring life in this bare, chilly landscape, and she was standing at its edge!

She made to creep forward, her eyes searching the firelit figures for the boy. But Hahn pulled her back, fingers to his lips.

"They'll hear you if you even breathe," he whispered. "Believe me."

Suddenly, Hahn pointed. Frankie looked and held quite still.

Sky-fire-trail.

Not by the fire, nor near any of the village folk. Only two

dozen paces from them, he was creeping forward, intent on the flames.

Signaling Frankie to stay put, Hahn raised a foot and took a cautious step through the snow.

Sky-fire-trail's head whipped around. For one instant he stood motionless, looking straight at them, then brightness flashed in his fingers.

Oh, no, thought Frankie. He was taking off again. She leapt and bounced like a porpoise through the snow, then bracing herself, she threw herself up and forward, and grabbed the boy's ankles in the greatest flying leap of her career.

"No!" Hahn shouted, but too late. The air shimmered, and crackled, and she was away, hanging on for her life.

Frankie opened her eyes on Broad Street, 1789. She was lying full length in the middle of the road, her arms stretched in front of her, hands still locked on Sky-fire-trail's ankles.

Sky-fire-trail kicked hard to break free, but Frankie held on.

He tried harder, straining Frankie's arms in their sockets, yet she dared not let go, for if he disappeared without her now, she'd be lost for sure. He kicked again, and Frankie felt her fingers give. Only a matter of time, she thought, before her hands tired and he broke free—unless she could turn things around.

"Okay, Frankie: what are our three options in karate?"

"Evasion, control, immobilization, in that order . . . If someone strikes, don't be there. Failing that, go for control . . . put your attacker on the defensive, passing the initiative to you."

Releasing her grip on Sky-fire-trail's ankles, Frankie threw herself forward, seized his right arm and bent it up behind him with all her strength.

Sky-fire-trail cried out, and the time stone rolled from his unclenched fist, onto the roadway.

Frankie let go and snatched the crystal up, feeling its warmth from his hand. She sprang to her feet a breath ahead of Sky-fire-trail, who, scowling murderously, came up also, at the same time pulling a short, flint dagger from his belt. No chance to run, she thought, taking in the long, strong legs. Her only chance was to keep the initiative. She dropped into Joonbi stance, weighing her best move.

Sky-fire-trail sprang.

"Kihap!" Frankie spun, then leapt, aiming a perfect *twieo dollyo-chagi*—jumping round house kick—at Sky-fire-trail's left shoulder. A moment later, the boy lay winded on his back, arms outflung, his stone knife skidding out of reach.

She'd decked him!

Frankie's knees started to tremble. All those hours, all that practice.

"Never enough." She could hear Mr. Ho now. *"Think: one day all this work might save your life!"*

Frankie glanced from Sky-fire-trail to his lost knife. Had she time to go for it, retrieve it, or maybe kick it farther out of reach? The shake in her knees spread all over.

Across the road, directly opposite, were the bushes where she'd stood with Hahn. At the end of the street to her left squatted Federal Hall, like some august family elder presiding at the head of the dinner table. To her right the other way, the gang of boys still waged their noisy game.

What to do? Frankie weighed the time stone, thinking rapidly. She couldn't use it, for she didn't know how it worked. But she had to make some move, fast. She eyed the boys dubiously. Were she and Sky-fire-trail visible? Surely, for they'd fully materialized. She felt threatened at the thought. One thing to peek in on these times and places from the protection of the ship. Quite another to be out here, exposed and fully solid in this space and time! Those boys looked tough, sounded every bit as tough as any street gang she'd seen on TV. What if they spotted her and Sky-fire-trail, and decided to join the fun?

Frankie turned from them and started out in the opposite direction, toward Federal Hall. Behind her, Sky-fire-trail was up and scrabbling in the roadway to retrieve his knife.

Suddenly came a shout. "Hey, what's he doing here!"

"Some nerve, showing his face. Who does he think he is!"

"A crazy, for sure—look at that hair!"

"Don't look like one of the locals. . . ."

"Ain't no Kinarsee, ain't no Manhattan, neither, not gotten up like that. Ain't from 'round these parts!"

"I seen him before, I think. Hey—you! C'm'ere! Let's look at you! Hey—'ere, we said!"

The ruckus grew: shouts, jeers, and catcalls, mingled with whoops. Frankie slowed, looking back. The boys were bearing down on Sky-fire-trail, who, seeing that, was standing, minus knife, braced to face them.

Passing grown-ups were stopping to watch the coming confrontation, making no move to stop the youths. In fact, a couple of men were egging them on. Frankie stood, appalled.

Sky-fire-trail was in trouble, for sure, and who would lift a finger to stop it?

How to draw him away? She couldn't see him running from anyone. "Hey!" she called, and held up the time stone to the sunlight.

Sky-fire-trail started after her.

She raced on to the street corner, and paused. Which way now? To her left, the way led to a church that looked as though it had come through a terrible fire. To her right, the street seemed to offer more space to run. Frankie went right, threading her way among handcarts, carriages, people on horseback, and pedestrians crossing over.

She dared not slow to look back. Sky-fire-trail must be gaining fast, she could hear his noisy retinue rounding the street corner. From just behind her came a sharp *chk,* and a rock skidded forward along the roadway in front of her. She glanced back. The youths were throwing stuff hard and fast, and not pebbles, either. People scattered right and left, leaving the flying stones clear path to Sky-fire-trail. One of the rocks had already hit, she could see blood on his cheek.

On, Frankie urged herself. Keep him coming after you! She picked up speed, tightening her fist about the time stone. To think that she and the boy could be out of all this in a flash—if only she knew how to use it. Sky-fire-trail knew. Dare she slow up, hand the crystal over? He was gaining on her; she could hear him.

If she was going to hand it over, best to stop, in case they fumbled and dropped the stone. Frankie looked from side to side for an opening, saw trim little shops with hanging wooden signs advertising grocer, saddler, and, there, in bright, gold letters, ROBERT LYLBYRNE, MERCHANT; 25 WALL STREET.

Wall Street! Then that church behind her was Trinity Church! Yes, hadn't Mom told her how it had been badly damaged in the fires of 1776 and 1778; and how the whole of Broadway, from Trinity Church right down to the Battery, was in ruins at the time of Washington's inauguration! Frankie pictured the Wall Street she knew: solid, squat buildings, skyscrapers seeming to squeeze church and cemetery into a tight little space. Her hand began to tingle. The tingle spread up her arm, through her body. She heard a faint crackling in her head, and the warm sunlit buildings began to dissolve in a bright haze.

She was beginning to dematerialize!

So that was how the stone worked! Simple, but effective. Very effective! In another moment, she'd have transmatted out. But what of Sky-fire-trail?

She turned to look at him through haze, and the sight of his set and bloodied face steadied her mind. The sunlight came back, the haze cleared, and the tingling faded to a faint prickle in her palm. Sweat broke out all over. That had been close. What a powerful stone this was. The trick was not how to use it, but how *not* to.

How long had passed? Seconds, her watch said, but it felt like hours. Her throat was salty, and pain stabbed her left side. She couldn't go on much longer. If only she could stop to collect her thought. And call a truce with Sky-fire-trail. Fat chance! He didn't know who she was, or what she wanted.

A few doors farther down the street, at number twenty-eight, was a tavern by an alley. PROPRIETOR, WILLIAM VANDRILL, the painted sign said, in neat gold letters over the door. She dodged down the alley, Sky-fire-trail at her heels. Behind the tavern was a dirt yard lined with stables and several sheds. Frankie ducked into the first shed, Sky-fire-trail after her.

They shut the door behind them, dove for the back wall, and wriggled into a pile of hay just as the youths burst into the yard.

She almost sat up again.

Far from escaping, she and Sky-fire-trail had only boxed themselves up for delivery! In another minute the place would be swarming with bodies, poking, prodding the straw inside, and no way out.

From the yard came a man's angry voice. "Here, here! Where do you think you're going? Get away!"

Frankie breathed out. "Bless you, William Vandrill," she whispered.

"There's a redskin in your yard, mister! He just come in your gate."

"Redskin? There ain't bin no redskin in this yard that I knows of—but there will be if I takes my stick to them backsides! Now—get out of here!"

The urchins jeered and shouted; about the redskin, and what they wouldn't do to him when they caught him, about how mean the man was, and what they wouldn't do to him if ever they got him down a dark alley.

Vandrill's voice rose to a full roar. There came the sound of a slap, a cry, and the gate slammed shut. Then all was quiet.

Redskin.

Frankie lay stunned. One moment, she and Sky-fire-trail had been standing on the edge of his village and the next, on almost that very same spot, he was being hunted down! A wave of shame swept over her, for the boys, and strangely, for herself. She wanted to speak, to say something, but remembering how he'd drawn his knife on her decided now was not the time. Instead, she rolled away under the straw, meaning to stand up a safe distance away. But quick as a whip, Sky-fire-trail caught her wrist, and held her fast. She began to struggle, to resist, but Sky-fire-trail only shook her arm and hissed at her to be still. Boots were crunching back toward them over the cobbled yard. The door latch scraped up with a rusty iron sound. Sunlight flooded the open door and a man poked his head in.

Vandrill. Frankie held her breath. Having second thoughts about the redskin in his yard? He cocked his head, listening. From beyond came the click of hooves on cobbles, the clank of a pail. With a shrug, Vandrill reached down a pitchfork from a rackful by the door, jabbed up a fork of hay, and went out.

Frankie stood up slowly, hand to her middle. The way that man had stabbed the hay with the fork!

Sky-fire-trail came up also, watching her. A shaft of sunlight slicing through the rough shed wall lit the planes of his face, the gleam of his eyes.

"You—Spirit Who Leaps With High Kick; Warrior Spirit: give me back the stone."

Spirit Who Leaps With High Kick? Warrior Spirit! He thought her a *spirit?* Maybe, but it didn't seem to faze him. She'd just been about to thank him for holding her down, but now, instead, she raised the time crystal defensively. "You make one move and I'm gone." Stupid, even to think of connecting with this guy, Frankie told herself in disgust. But she couldn't ditch him. "Listen, Hahn's got trouble," she said. "We have to find him fast."

"No." Sky-fire-trail shook his head. "Hahn-spirit will punish me. There is bad blood between us."

"There's nothing of the sort. Hahn couldn't wish ill to a fly. Now listen, we have to get out of here. And that means, well, holding on. So swear you'll not harm me, or try to take this stone from me."

Sky-fire-trail fixed his eyes on her with exaggerated innocence. "Who would dare to pit himself against such as Warrior Spirit?"

"You would," she snapped.

Sky-fire-trail drew himself up. "A man's word is his bond."

"So swear." She shook the stone at him.

"That I will not."

Sky-fire-trail folded his arms, eyeing the small one critically: the pale face, the short, dark hair tipped with light. Though she was spirit like Hahn, for all her strength, she was not as powerful, he reasoned, seeing now the band-of-many-tongues like his. Yet . . . she was one with those many future faces, part of the calamity that would destroy the land, his people, his whole way of life.

His brows came together. One with those cowards who'd thrown rocks at him, hunting him down as beast.

He fingered the cut on his cheekbone. The flesh was

swollen, but the flow had stopped, leaving a smear of caked blood down his cheek. Blood that must be paid for—but not by this small spirit. His face cleared. She might look like those others, but she was not really of them. She had fled them, drawing him from that confrontation. And he had withdrawn from injury, maybe death, without losing honor.

He eyed her speculatively. She had the stone. Why hadn't she gone, leaving him here? And why had she saved him from that crowd? To deliver him up to Hahn-spirit for punishment? His face darkened again. Well, she'd deliver neither him nor the stone for he was going to get it back. He must make bargain with Hahn-spirit!

He reached automatically for his knife. Not there, of course. Left behind on that wide, bright trail. He crouched to spring. In answer, Warrior Spirit raised the crystal. He straightened slowly. Better to be cunning, think like a hunter. "You have great skill, Warrior Spirit. How did you do that?" He clumsily mimed her kick.

Warrior Spirit laughed. "I learned it in karate class."

"Ka-ra-te?" The strange word had come through whole via his translator. "What is that?"

"A school of *self-defense.*"

"Ah." He nodded, hearing a word he well knew. "*Wrestling.*" That didn't prove she wasn't spirit.

She held out her arm. "Let's go."

Sky-fire-trail drew back. He didn't want to go with her. He wanted that stone! He discarded the friendly approach, was preparing to spring again, when the air between them darkened, and a great shape began to form.

"Hahn!" Warrior Spirit ran forward eagerly as the shape solidified, but as Sky-fire-trail watched, the great one seized her and slammed her against the shed wall with such force that she fell to the floor. Sky-fire-trail stood, stunned. Such anger! Had he not been right to fear Hahn-spirit, despite the friendliness? If Hahn-spirit could do that to his own kind, what might he now do with just cause to Sky-fire-trail? He dropped into a half crouch, braced to defend himself.

But as the giant came at him, Warrior Spirit cried out.

"Back off! Back off, Sky-fire-trail! That's not Hahn!"

A hand lashed out, seized him by the throat. Sky-fire-trail struck out wildly, snatched empty air. He struggled for breath, sparks pricking his vision. He thrashed about with all his might, but Hahn-spirit did not waver. Such strength there was in that one! Where was *she?* Standing by, watching Hahn-spirit end this feud? Angry pride gave him fresh, brief power to resist, but his struggles weakened. Patches of dark blocked out the sparks, multiplied, and flowed together . . .

All at once, with a loud cry, the huge hand let go his windpipe, and the giant figure toppled heavily to the floor. Sky-fire-trail thudded onto his knees, his hands to his throat, his laboring breath hot and raw.

Warrior Spirit shook his shoulder. "Sky-fire-trail—get up—quick!" She stood over him, holding a pitchfork. "I hit him with the handle. But it won't last. Quick, before—"

The great one stirred and looked up. Warrior Spirit dropped the pitchfork and backed off to stand by the wall, her dark eyes wide. Hahn-spirit raised a red-sleeved arm and pointed his finger. Warrior Spirit cried out, and rolled.

A ball of fire hit the wall where she'd been standing. Sky-fire-trail saw the round charred hole, smelled hot, resinous wood. Before Sky-fire-trail could move, Hahn-spirit leapt up and raised his arm toward the smaller spirit a second time.

"Leap! Warrior Spirit, leap and kick!" Sky-fire-trail found himself shouting, but Warrior Spirit only squeezed up her eyes and turned her head away.

Frankie braced herself for the hit, wondering in that long second how bad it would feel and, oddly, sorry she'd not see Mom again. But instead of pain, there came the strangest sound, a kind of squeal, as of a stuck wild animal. She looked up.

Un-Hahn lay in the straw, face down. Behind him, eyes wide, nostrils flared, stood Sky-fire-trail, holding the pitch-fork, prongs down. But he didn't look happy at all. "He saved me, and now I have destroyed him."

"That's not Hahn!" Frankie scrambled up, and stepped around Un-Hahn's inert body. "It truly isn't, you'll see." Would Hahn still be in the village? Hardly. He'd have gone back to the ship to scan for them. She held out her arm. "Come on, take hold. We must get out of here."

"Where?" Sky-fire-trail eyed her guardedly.

"Well, I guess I'll take you home."

Sky-fire-trail looked down at the still figure. "Very well." He closed his fingers about her arm.

Frankie shut her eyes, then opened them again. What if she didn't do it right? Sky-fire-trail was watching expectantly.

Her chin came up. He could do it, so could she. She pictured the shelters huddled darkly under the full moon, flames flickering against the night sky, and glistening snow.

The tingling started, and the sparks came. Out there, the solid world was coming apart, dissolving, spilling her out. She pulled back, afraid, and at once the shed began to reform. Feet away from where she stood, Un-Hahn opened his eyes and raised his hand toward her.

Frankie squeezed her eyes shut, and thought of the Indian village.

Icy wind stripped away her fragile layers of warmth.

Shuddering, Frankie opened her eyes, found herself with Sky-fire-trail behind the tipis where they'd left Hahn. She let go of Sky-fire-trail and looked around. No sign of Hahn, but then she hadn't expected it. He'd gone back to his ship, surely, to scan for them. She must catch him, before the two of them started chasing each other in circles.

"Well," she whispered. "Here you are." She waited for him to go.

He clapped a hand to his belt. "My knife!" he said. "I left behind my knife!"

"Too bad," she said. "Wild horses wouldn't take me back to that place. You'll have to make another. Good-bye."

"Not good-bye." Sky-fire-trail folded his arms, looking down severely. "Now Hahn-spirit is destroyed, you shall help me instead."

"What! Are you crazy?" Frankie puffed out in exasperation. "Look, I got you home, didn't I? So good-bye, and good luck." She raised her hand in valedictory salute, thinking, some neat guy, and what a friend he'd have made, even as she closed her eyes to picture Hahn's ship, Hahn at the controls.

As the air began to crackle, strong fingers gripped her arm, and Sky-fire-trail's voice sounded in her ear. "Until you've helped me save my people, I stay with you: see."

Frankie opened her eyes wide. "No! You must stay here where you bel—"

She never finished.

Hahn lay sprawled across the cabin floor.

Frankie jammed the time stone in her pocket, and rushed to his side. She lifted the large, heavy head, turned the face up toward her. "Oh, Hahn!" His eyes were closed. One cheek was crushed, and clear fluid oozed like tree-sap. She looked around in shock at the ruined cabin. Half the lights were gone, smashed. The floor was strewn with colored crystal. The monitors were dark and dead. The walls were pocked and dented, holed in places.

Frankie looked across at Sky-fire-trail. "Now do you believe me?" she said. Sky-fire-trail stayed still; silent, wary. She looked down, reached to feel Hahn's neck, then remembering he had no pulse, straightened up again. Was Hahn dead? How could she know? She glanced to the LSRM. That, at least, looked undamaged.

"He is destroyed?"

"How do I know?" Frankie put her hands under Hahn's

arms, and heaved, and as she did so, Sky-fire-trail bent down, inspecting Hahn's back. She got Hahn up a little way, then had to let him fall. She looked at Sky-fire-trail in exasperation. "Don't just stand there. Help me raise him."

Sky-fire-trail came around to Hahn's head, looking puzzled. "There were no marks in Hahn-spirit's back. I believe you now, although—ah." His face cleared. "The one we left in the shed was Hahn-spirit's enemy: the one who seeks him." He looked down. "Twin spirits, one good; the other, evil. Well, now the evil one is destroyed, and my debt, repaid."

"Don't bet on that," Frankie muttered, remembering how Un-Hahn had fixed himself the last time. "Are you going to help or not!" she demanded, then exclaimed, "What am I doing?" She hadn't yet raised the LSRM lid.

She ran around to the control panel, dreading to see it smashed. Looked okay. Cautiously, she pressed the green crystal. The light winked on, and the lid came slowly up.

"You can work the healing canoe?" Sky-fire-trail actually smiled. "You, Warrior Spirit, are shaman spirit also."

With great care and effort, they lifted Hahn, and swung him up and into the LSRM to lie on his back—no easy matter. At every shift, Frankie heard crunching and cracking inside his great body. Was he himself aware? Did he hurt? Or was he damaged beyond repair? Only time would tell.

She arranged his long arms by his sides, just as she'd seen him do the last time, and fitted the cap to his head. Then, bending down, she touched the crystals in the order Hahn had taught her: purple, yellow, violet, and orange, then lastly, the green once more. Side by side, she and Sky-fire-trail watched the lid go down. Had she done right?

If not, if Hahn were injured beyond repair . . . Frankie glanced to the dark infinity stone set into the wall.

"Just suppose Un-Hahn had beaten you. . . ?

. . . he would gather up evidence of my visit and delete it."

It occurred to Frankie then that Un-Hahn had had that chance to ditch Hahn and the ship. But both were still here. She frowned, sensing some catch. Why? She slid her hand into her pocket, took out the time stone. Because of this? A loose end, they called it, on Earth. Back in the shed, she'd assumed Un-Hahn had locked onto it thinking them Hahn. But now it looked as though he'd left Hahn to fetch the last shred of evidence; to make a clean sweep before sending pilot and ship, bag and baggage, to infinity.

Why, she realized now, if Sky-fire-trail hadn't stolen this stone, Hahn would already be on his way to nowhere; and Earth, in certain jeopardy. She recalled the sight of Un-Hahn stirring as she vanished from the shed, and wondered grimly where he was now.

Sky-fire-trail's voice startled her. "Be glad, Warrior Spirit. You, at least, survived your feud with the Bad One."

"I guess." Frankie stared around the cabin, wondering what to do. They ought to go somewhere, certainly, out of Un-Hahn's reach, keeping his attention, and at the same time giving Hahn chance to heal. "Sky-fire-trail, we should think about getting—"

The air between began to turn dark.

Sky-fire-trail leapt up, reached for his vanished knife, then moved to stand beside her just as the shape of Un-Hahn began to form. Go! go! go! Frankie's mind screamed, but where?

Un-Hahn had almost materialized. Only seconds left to decide. *Where, oh, where?*

Aunt Maggie's farm! No people, and space all around. Seizing Sky-fire-trail's arm, Frankie pictured them standing in Aunt Maggie's back yard, facing the rickety porch, barn on her right, split rails behind her, gap leading down to the lake. Cricket and Jocko would be leaping for her shoulder, licking her face.

Go! Go! *GO!*

Un-Hahn was coming at them when the crystal flared, blocking him out.

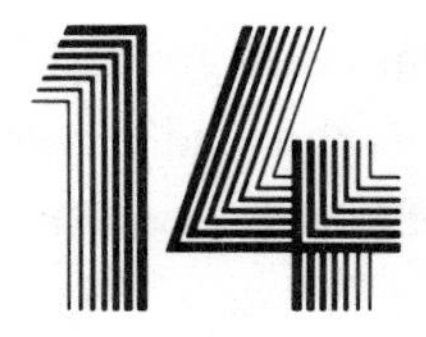

The moment the haze cleared, the great beasts leapt.

Sky-fire-trail crouched, eyes wary, hand still to his empty belt.

''Down, Cricket, down, Jocko!'' Frankie thrust her hands before her to fend them off. They didn't listen, naturally, but took it in turns, first Cricket, then Jocko, to rest their paws on her shoulders, sending her staggering backward, smothering her cheek with rough, wet licks, while the free one investigated Sky-fire-trail, snuffing and wagging its tail.

Sky-fire-trail came up slowly, then stood very still. Did they have tame dogs in his time? They had wolves, Frankie knew.

''It's okay,'' she said. ''They're friendly.''

''Hm.'' He didn't sound convinced.

Frankie broke free, glanced at her watch. One-thirty-five. Uncle Jim and Aunt Maggie would have taken the old Chevy truck into town for their regular weekly shopping trip and wouldn't be back until three.

"It's all right," she said to Sky-fire-trail. "This place belongs to some of my family. We're safe here as anywhere. And they're away for now." She led Sky-fire-trail across the yard to the back door, unlocked, of course. This was not the big city. She stepped through the tilting back porch into the kitchen, catching at once the old familiar odors: aged wood, green soap, paraffin oil, mothballs, linoleum. A flowered bowl of African violets graced the red-and-white checkered table cloth. The faded walls were patched with bright calendars, never mind the year: the Canadian Rockies, long shot of Montreal, aerial shot of the Sierra Nevada, close-up of an alligator snout poking from a bayou in the Everglades; a tram climbing a steep San Francisco street with a man in jeans and T-shirt in the act of jumping off; the Horseshoe Falls, and the Banff railway station after a snowstorm. Aunt Maggie's favorite pictures from each calendar, regardless of the month.

Sky-fire-trail, still by the door, warily taking it all in, leapt back as the ancient Frigidaire turned over with its usual cough and grunt.

"Are you thirsty?" Frankie crossed quickly to the old porcelain sink under the window, and reaching down two tumblers from the overhead shelf, filled them with water.

Sky-fire-trail padded across the blue linoleum floor, intent on the whole process. She caught his expression, guessed his thought, and smiled to herself. When would he get it into his mind that she was no spirit? To him, there'd be no difference between summoning water out of Hahn's wall and Aunt Maggie's spicket!

It occurred to her that he'd never seen a tumbler before.

She held up her own, rolled it between her open palms, feeling its cold hardness. Why, the glass itself must look like ice to him. Sure enough, he flicked his fingernail against it, then scratched it. Frost formed on the outside of her glass, and beading, trickled down its sides. She held the glass to the light and looked through it.

To her surprise, Sky-fire-trail did the same. His eye through the glass looked large and dark; the lashes, thick and long. She turned her head away, uncomfortably aware of him, and his closeness.

Sky-fire-trail, seemingly quite innocent of her turn of thought, lowered his glass also, and drank.

He held out his empty tumbler. "What is this?"

"Glass," she said.

" 'Glass'?" He looked to her doubtfully. Then he nodded in sudden understanding. "Ah, spirit-ice that does not melt."

"Oh. But it's not—" Frankie began, then, shrugging, let it go. As Hahn had warned, the translator band sure had its dangers. She took his empty tumbler, put it with hers into the sink, and gazed out across the yard, over the split cedar fence, toward the lake.

Last summer she'd spent days fishing out there with Uncle Jim, and some evenings, Aunt Maggie had invited the Weekes from the next farm to share their catch around the rusty old barbecue in the back yard: the two senior Weekes and their two children, Jed, who was Frankie's own age, and Emily, one year their senior. They'd all three played together forever. Frankie had liked them a lot, until a couple of summers back when Emily had suddenly gotten much older, and talked of nothing but boys. And Jed, too, had somehow lost his spark. What, she wondered, would they make of Sky-fire-trail—or he of them?

Frankie looked at the glasses in the sink. What was she doing!

She imagined Aunt Maggie coming in loaded with the shopping bags and finding her suddenly there. How could Frankie possibly explain her presence? Or Sky-fire-trail's? And what if Un-Hahn located them, what kind of trouble would she have brought home to Aunt Maggie and Uncle Jim?

Frankie turned back to the room.

Sky-fire-trail was pussyfooting around, picking things up and putting them down again with great precision, running his lean fingers over everything, even the old willow chairs.

They couldn't stay there.

So now where could she and Sky-fire-trail go so's not to cause Aunt Maggie any trouble? She thought of the lake. Yes, that was it. They'd go there, then back in time, maybe, to Sky-fire-trail's own era. Far enough.

But first she rinsed the glasses, replaced them on the shelf. Then she crossed to the fridge, opened the door, and took out a slab of yellow cheese. She cut two fair-sized hunks off it, one for her, one for Sky-fire-trail.

"What is that?"

"Cheddar."

He eyed it with interest. "Ched-dar. What is ched-dar?"

"Cheese," Frankie replied, and wondered at once how that had come through his translator band. According to

Bingham Webb, the Delaware Indians hadn't kept dairy herds, so the boy had probably never seen anything like that, either. She cut a sliver for him to taste. ''Cheese,'' she repeated, carefully, and waited.

He looked at it, puzzled. ''Milk-food? This doesn't look like milk.'' He took a bite, nodded in satisfaction. ''Where do you get this milk-food? And how do you make it like this?''

''We get the milk from a cow,'' she told him, then rolled up her eyes in despair. ''A sort of . . . momma moose,'' she said. ''You take her milk, you warm it, then you add some kind of acid to make it coagulate—'' Frankie gave up. She really did know how all kinds of cheeses were made, from an old dogeared *Henley's Formulas* on her mother's bottom bookshelf, but what use was that when her words were probably going through Sky-fire-trail's band like spaghetti?

She looked up, found him eyeing her in a most peculiar fashion.

''Ice that doesn't melt. Milk you bite on,'' he said, when it was obvious she'd given up. ''The spirit world is indeed strange. But this is good. *Ched-dar*. I like it.''

Mollified, Frankie got on with gathering supplies. To the cheese she added slabs of whole wheat bread, a couple of large green Granny Smiths, and stuffed them all into a brown paper grocery bag. ''Let's go.''

They were halfway to the fence when she stopped, eyeing Sky-fire-trail's empty belt. ''Wait.'' She shoved the bag at him, then ran to the barn at the side of the house. It was dark inside, and cobwebby, and the air smelled of creosote and gasoline. She walked around the tractor to the bench by the far wall where Uncle Jim kept his fishing gear. There, beside Uncle Jim's big tackle box, was her own, smaller one. She opened it, drew out a handsome red-handled knife in a thick leather sheath, decorated with—she grinned wryly—the profile of a stern sachem in a beaded eagle bonnet that reached all the way down to his feet. She closed the box, replaced it, and moved back to the barn door. She was almost there, when she stopped. Was she making a mistake? Sky-fire-trail no doubt was still after the stone, to regain power over her, and probably wouldn't hesitate to get it back at any cost.

She weighed the knife in her hands. Saw once more the dripping pitchfork prongs. Hadn't he saved her life? Besides, he expected her to help him. So he wouldn't snatch the stone and ditch her. Wouldn't hurt her now. She went out, closing the barn door behind her.

"Here." Frankie held out the knife.

Sky-fire-trail set down the paper bag, reached out and took her offering. Slowly, he examined the leather tooling, traced the chief's face reverently with his finger. Evidently, he understood what the lines signified. Then grasping the bright red plastic hilt, he slid the knife from the sheath, and slowly turned it over and over.

The blade caught the sunlight, flashed in her eyes. *Bethlehem Steel,* it said, up near the handle, she knew that so well, though she couldn't see through the glare.

Sky-fire-trail felt the blade edge delicately between thumb and forefinger, then looked up, something like wonder on his face. "You . . . give this . . . to me?"

She nodded, her crossed fingers tightening.

He raised it like some ancient knight pledging his sword.

"Thank you. If the hunter comes again, this blade shall greet him."

Uncomfortably aware of their closeness again, so much so now that her fingers trembled, Frankie showed Sky-fire-trail how to attach the sheath onto his belt, fumbling the thongs and bungling the knots. As he resettled his blanket over his shoulder, she turned away smartly and leapt the fence, bag and all.

"Let's go," she said, and without a backward glance, strode off at a lick in the teeth of the wind, through the winding hill gap toward the lake, her burning face averted.

An icy breeze sliced in over the water, making Frankie shiver. The Laurentians were invisible behind a haze of chilly mist. Spring came later this far north; the trees on the hillsides were still bare. She led the way along the bank to a sandy inlet through which flowed a little sheltered creek, so sheltered, in fact, that there was a small cave set in the left-hand bank. She led the way along the narrow, sandy spit between creek and lake, then going off a little by herself, she took out the time stone and stood staring thoughtfully down at it. Under the chill sunlight she fancied she saw fine silvery wires criss-crossing through the crystal in all directions, without touching. It seemed to radiate warmth. *Energy.* Was it solar-powered, perhaps?

Whatever, she was going to make it take them back to Sky-fire-trail's day—but how? She'd never seen this place as it was then, so she couldn't very well picture it. Sky-fire-trail would make a much better job of it. Should she hand over the stone? She eyed him doubtfully, decided not to risk it. She would instead try imaging the lake, at the same time thinking, *back to Sky-fire-trail's time*. Yes. That might work. With a show of confidence that she didn't feel, she held out her arm.

"Hold on," she said. "We're going back to your day." She clutched the stone tightly with her other hand and closed her eyes.

Frankie felt the shock of it almost at once: swiftly running water, soaking through her jeans, swishing past her knees. She opened her eyes to find herself standing, not beside the creek now, but in it, with the sand spit to her left as she faced the shore.

She stood, confused, while rushy currents tugged at her legs. This was where they'd been standing? How could it be? Beside her, Sky-fire-trail sniffed the air, drew in a deep lungful of it, and seemed to loosen some.

"What happened?" Frankie murmured, looking about. "I don't see—oh." There was the cave mouth, exactly where it had been a moment ago in relation to where they were standing. There'd been no mistake. This must be the very same spot. And the creek would be following an older course. Rivers shifted all the time—the Mississippi often overnight. Reassured, Frankie relaxed and sniffed the air as Sky-fire-trail had done. Mmmm. It had a moist green smell, of fern, and leaf mold, and rich, rotted humus. The trees were in leaf, and . . . she idly flapped away some large-winged insect . . .

it was warm—hot, even. When she brought them here, she must unconsciously have been wishing for kinder weather! But what a shock, after expecting to find familiar ground, to come out on alien territory. When Sky-fire-trail had emerged onto Broad Street those times—it must have been a shock for him, too. And much worse than hers, she thought, somberly, gazing around. Instead of open pasture, spindly saplings twisted out of moist, fern floor back to the foothills beyond. And behind them, dark green virgin forest spread even farther, to misty mountains, as far as the eye could see.

Beautiful, and quite mysterious in its difference.

Oh, well, they couldn't stand there forever. "Come on," she said, and began to wade toward the bank, but Sky-fire-trail caught her arm and pulled her back. New knife in hand, he slowly scanned the margin of the lake, and the territory beyond. "Follow me, and keep close," he said at last.

He led the way to the bank and on to the cave mouth. Frankie didn't mind. This was no longer her place, where she lay and sunbathed, where she floated idly in the little dinghy with Uncle Jim, their fishing lines trailing down through the limpid currents. The whole place looked, smelled—*felt*—so unfamiliar, she might well have been on some other planet.

"Wait here," Sky-fire-trail said, leaving her beside the cave.

She watched him walk away along the shore, his back receding, until, suddenly, he pulled up and bent down to inspect the sand. What was it? She longed to ask but he was too far away and she dared not shout. Without a glance in her direction, he came up again, peering out into the trees. Then, without warning, he struck off into them, and disappeared.

Frankie waited: one minute, two. At least, that's what her watch said, but it seemed longer. She shifted uneasily, becoming aware now of the leaves rustling among the trees, the lap of the lake water against the shore . . .

A loud sound cracked the air, like mad laughter, coming from the lake. Frankie whipped around. Way out, in the middle of the open water, a small, dark dot bobbed with the waves. She clutched her chest, and released her breath. A loon. She should have known, should have recognized that call, being well used to hearing it. But here, in this alien landscape, that familiar, maniacal call sounded different, even sinister. She watched the bird turning around and around, waiting for her heartbeat and the thudding in her ears to subside.

Somewhere behind her, a twig snapped. Frankie spun about to face the shore, expecting Sky-fire-trail to step out from the trees.

Nothing.

That had been something, or someone. If not him, then who? He'd been gone too long. Had he met with some accident—or worse? What, she thought, her unease growing, if he never came back?

She shaded her eyes, looking along the shore, and—there he was, walking calmly toward her. She almost ran to meet him. "Aren't you the least bit scared," she said. "In all this wild?"

"Wild?" He looked puzzled. "What is *wild?*"

"All this around us," she said, then realized. For Sky-fire-trail, there was no 'wild' for there was no 'tamed' land to set it apart. Ornamental gardens, manicured parklands, and trimmed lawns: these products of so-called civilization were outside his experience. If she read Sky-fire-trail right, he'd have no stomach for such places.

"I found tracks of wolf and moose," he said, "but days old. Fresh spoor of muskrat and otter. Waterfowl. No men, that I can see." He gestured behind them toward the Laurentians, invisible from where they now stood. "There was fire back near the foothills. It burned fiercely for many days. All the deadfall in that area is gone to ash, still warm in places." He pointed out a faint plume of smoke rising above the treetops. "The fire still smolders yonder," he said. "Let's hope the wind stays friendly while we are here. There was another, bigger one some moons ago, coming all the way down to the lake. That is why these trees around us are so young."

Frankie frowned, thinking of Smokey Bear. Forest fires were man-made, weren't they? "Who caused them?"

"Why, no one." He seemed surprised at the question. "Fire often comes during the hot season. It mostly starts when lightning strikes brittle deadwood. This is how land and forest renew themselves. This place is full of such tinder."

Frankie stood uncertainly. Maybe it hadn't been such a great idea to come to this place, or, rather, time, she thought, but Sky-fire-trail, looking quite at home, strode off along the shore toward the dark cave mouth.

She followed. Here, at least, was one place she should know. The small round cavern with the rock ledge where she dumped her picnic pack on hot afternoons while she tramped over the open pastures to the wooded foothills and back. She ducked her head under the low entrance, to find no small cavern at all, but a tunnel, going back under the bank.

Frankie stepped into the tunnel, moving forward slowly until it dwindled to a crack. All around her, almost touching her hair, her shoulders, great seams split the tunnel walls, and roof, some wide enough to thrust her hand in. Overhead, one giant wedge between two seams looked poised to come down any moment. . . . She backed hastily. There must have been many rock falls between this and her time. That's why the cave had grown so much smaller. She retreated into the daylight, glad to leave behind the clammy smell of rock and take a breath of outside air.

It had grown hotter out here, at least, seemed like it. Hotter than when Frankie had gone into the cavern. She peeled off her jacket, pushed up the sleeves of her red sweater. Along the open shore, the sun burned the sand, reflected off the lake surface, dazzling her eyes.

No sign of the loon.

Sweat started on Frankie's forehead under the translator band. She took off her wet socks and sneakers, rinsed them and set them out to dry, then rolled up her jeans to the knee. Sky-fire-trail, meanwhile, emerging from the cave, sat himself down, took out his new knife, and turned it over, admiring the flash of the blade in the sunlight.

Frankie looked at her watch. Two-fifteen. How long should they stay there? Hahn might well take longer to heal than before, being so badly injured. She took out the food, tore the paper bag in two, split everything into two equal shares, and set Sky-fire-trail's by his side. "Dig in," she said. "I'm starving."

With a nod, Sky-fire-trail set down his knife and picked up his Granny Smith. "What is this?"

"An apple," she said in surprise. "Didn't you have apples in your day?"

"Certainly," he said, turning it over in his hands. "I know apples. But they are small, dry, and full of worm. This green spirit-apple is as big as a whole harvest." He sniffed it, took a cautious nibble, and smiled in delight. "Our apples taste bitter. This," he went on, taking a hearty bite now, and splattering juice all over, "is sweet as nectar."

Frankie helped herself to bread and cheese thoughtfully. Weird, the way his mouth formed one word, while the translator band said something else. Like how just now, as he spoke, she had heard 'apple,' while his mouth had formed a different sound. Like in a foreign movie with dubbing. On a sudden idea, she scooped up a handful of sand. "What is this?" she asked, watching his mouth.

"Earth," his voice came through the translator. But his lips formed quite another name.

Frankie slipped off her band. "Say that again."

"Reckwa," he repeated.

"Reck-wa." She said the word with care. "Reckwa. And this?" She dropped the sand, took up a pebble.

"Assin."

"Assin," Frankie repeated. *Assin,* stone, pebble. She looked up along the lake shore. Several hundred yards away, the ground rose slightly, forming a low bank over the water. She pointed. "What would you call that rise along there?"

Sky-fire-trail followed her arm. "That? *Aquehung,*" he said.

''Aque-hung.'' Frankie slipped the band back on. ''Say it again.''

Sky-fire-trail obeyed, but this time Frankie heard the English, ''cliff.'' *Cliff?* She shot him a quick look, caught the glint in his eye. Why, he was teasing her! She tipped her chin up. ''Aquehung,'' she said doggedly.

Sky-fire-trail began to laugh. She looked at him in astonishment. This boy who rarely smiled—he was laughing at her! Frankie thought of a smart retort, but, glancing back to her little bank, she saw the fun of it. Now she began to laugh, and couldn't stop. So there they both sat, the pair of them, rocking back and forth with laughter.

As one, they straightened, caught each other's eye.

''Aquehung,'' they said, like a chorus, which sent them off again.

From now on, Frankie resolved, wiping her eyes, that modest rise was her soaring cliff, her *aquehung,* for ever and ever!

She finished off her apple, while Sky-fire-trail found a straight ash stick and with his new knife began whittling one end of it to a fine sharp point. He looked so *right* sitting there, intent on his task. As though he belonged. Frankie sighed. Descendant of the Woodland People. There he was, and there she was. And somewhere out there in space and time was a little patch of dirt, earth—*auke*—called Manhattan. And through some terrible, deadly game of musical chairs to be played between his descendants and her ancestors, his folk would drop off into nowhere. . . .

She sighed explosively.

There must be some way they could all win.

Sky-fire-trail got up, and walked along to her "aquehung," climbed atop it. Above the bank lay a large, round boulder, like a giant hamburger bun, good for sitting up against, or lying on to sunbathe. That stone was Frankie's favorite spot in the summer, a place where Aunt Maggie was almost sure to find her come supper time. Sky-fire-trail climbed atop that stone and stood with his back to the lake, staring up through the spindly trees, looking pretty much as he'd looked on the rock in Central Park.

A feeling started up somewhere, a strangeness that she'd never had before. It was as though she'd known him the longest time . . .

What would it be like, Frankie wondered, if they stayed there together, away from that whole mess. She pictured them swimming in the lake, sitting under the stars by a camp fire. Come winter, there was the cave, Sky-fire-trail would know how to make it right. And there they'd be, safe, making out okay for themselves.

Frankie made an impatient noise. What was she thinking of? She was taking them for some kind of teen Tarzan and Jane, or the two kids in *The Blue Lagoon,* living on some coral island, with no idea who they were or where they came from! This was no tropical paradise, but a small lake in an unforgiving northern latitude. And they were not two innocents growing up together, but practically adult, knowing perfectly well who they were, and where they belonged, and what the stakes were out there—right now.

She jumped up and followed Sky-fire-trail, climbing from

sandy shore onto soft fern and peat moss, and ash from the last forest fire. Reaching her rock, she climbed and stood beside him, her back also to the lake, gazing with him out over the tops of the saplings, up into the distance, noting the differences in that primal skyline from the one she knew.

Presently, he turned away. "The land is good. The lake churns with fish, and up among the hills is rich hunting ground."

"The winters are real bad," Frankie said. "The snows come over your head, and the wind freezes your ears off."

"Like home." Sky-fire-trail's face darkened.

"Oh, no," Frankie said. "Not like Manhattan. It drops to twenty below, up here."

"Twenty below? Below what?"

Frankie sighed and rolled her eyes. "It gets a whole bunch colder here than down south," she said. "That's what."

Sky-fire-trail leapt from the rock, then down off the bank, back toward the cave. Frankie stayed where she was, staring fixedly at the sunlight flashing on the lake. How had it happened, day by day, year by year? Where had they gone, his clan? The children, the children's children? And the trees, and all the wide green spaces that had been his Manhattan home?

Echoing silence pressed in upon her. From somewhere in the hills came a crow's hoarse cry. A fish flashed silver from the lake and fell back again with a soft plop. Still no sign of the loon.

How had he described the lake just now? *Churning with fish.* Like he wished he lived there. And she'd put him down, judging things from her point of view. Oh, sure, it was freezing up here in the winters: she wouldn't last a day—or night—out here on her own. But Sky-fire-trail?

That dumb daydream she'd just had—perhaps it hadn't been totally out of the ball park. What if, she thought, snatching a feathered grass and stroking it between her fingers, what if Sky-fire-trail could bring his people here? There was so much land, even now in Aunt Maggie's time. These Laurentian foothills were west of the Algonquins, inside Iroquois territory. The idea grew inside her, swelling to burst her chest.

"Sky-fire-trail!" She started down the bank, then checked. Could he do it? Could he pull it off? Was it possible? What did history say?

Frankie knew for a fact that Iroquois were there, and had a strong political voice in that whole region, right now, in Aunt Maggie's day. Yes! It would work, and no question in her mind that Sky-fire-trail could get his people up here. Why, he could do anything he set his mind to!

But would he?

He was very stubborn. And right now he considered only one solution to his trouble, was convinced that Hahn—or she—should kill the mammoth, not that he should get out of its way. She realized uncomfortably that perhaps he was not the only one with stubborn tendencies. "I'm the pot calling the kettle black," she murmured, thinking back to her last karate class.

"Stubborn Frankie, sticking with the same old options, even if they get you killed! How many times do I tell you—there's always more than one way out of trouble. Remember that, and we have real power: the power of choice."

Could she change his mind? She could at least try.

Frankie hurried to join him, carefully rehearsing her words.

Sky-fire-trail was lying back, the knife at his belt, the stick at his side, his eyes closed. "This is a land of good spirits," he murmured. "Where does it lie from my home?"

"Due north," Frankie said. She knelt beside him, seizing her chance. "Here. Lend me that stick."

Sky-fire-trail sat up, handed over his homemade spear.

Frankie took it, drew a fish in the sand. "Manhattan," she said, then poked a hole near its nose. "This is your village. To get up here, you cross the Hudson, and follow it all the way to this big lake."

She made a bulge in the river for Lake Champlain. "You'd go around the lake shore on the west side, until it becomes a river again. There, you'd leave the river and turn northwest," she moved the spear tip diagonally up to the left, "until another great river crosses your path." She sketched in the St. Lawrence, running up slantwise from left to right. "When you reach this big river, you should see a little mountain poking up in the middle of it. We call that 'Montreal' today." Frankie drew in the island, then moved the spear point to the left and up a little way.

"Just a minute," he said. "I asked you only where this place was, not how to get there."

"To reach where we are now from there," Frankie went on quickly, "you cross the river and then travel west-northwest across the valley floor until you see low hills in the distance. They're those blue hills yonder." She pointed up over the bank behind them. "There are many small lakes in this region. You'll have to search around for this actual one, but you'll know it when you see it, 'cause it's shaped like a running man. You can see that quite clearly from the hills back there,'' she said, then wondered if he would, now, through all the trees.

As she spoke, she drew the lake in anyway, completing the map in every detail, just as Mom had taught her one rainy afternoon in Aunt Maggie's kitchen summers ago. And when she had done, she sat back, and waited.

''I see.'' Sky-fire-trail studied the markings in the sand intently for some time. Then he looked up, a deep fold between his brows. ''Men have come to the village from time to time, hunters who have spoken of such a river with a high rock in the middle.'' He nodded thoughtfully. ''And so from there this place lies north, and into the setting sun.'' He slowly traced the sand markings with his fingers. ''How far?''

''Oh, it's close, very close,'' she said. ''It's—oh.'' She broke off. The words ''how far'' referred to two quite different journeys. Hers, in hours and miles by bus or car or train or plane. And that she could have told him exactly. His, in days or weeks or even months on foot, hacking a way up the Hudson Valley and across thick-wooded plain beyond. And if he meant what she hoped he meant, also encumbered by a whole community, lock, stock, and barrel: men, women, children; the young and the old—some of the latter maybe ill and infirm. There were trails, she recalled Webb saying. But no throughways, no comfort stations, with their fast-food counters, washrooms, and gas stations; no motels with comfortable beds to sleep in. It could take days, weeks, months, of hardship and tough going. ''It will take many moons on foot,'' she amended lamely. ''But a man could make the journey if he had a mind to.''

''Mm.'' Sky-fire-trail lay down again. ''Me, I'm happy where I am.''

''But for how long?'' she said, and bit her wayward tongue.

''Forever. If Hahn-spirit won't make the calamity go away, you shall.''

''I can't.''

Sky-fire-trail's brows came down. ''Are you not friendly?''

''Oh, heavens, we're friends, I should hope.''

''So? As friendly spirit, you would help us, surely?''

''Absolutely. But when I say, can't, I really mean, cannot. Look,'' she said, holding out her hands in appeal. ''May I give you some advice?''

''Say what it is.''

Frankie took courage. ''The trouble is, you're so darned stubborn.''

''Stubborn?'' Sky-fire-trail sat up slowly, his face darkening.

She hurried on. ''You get a certain notion in your head and that's it. You barge forward, expecting Hahn and me to do what you want, regardless of whether it's desirable, or even possible. And with no thought of compromise.''

Sky-fire-trail folded his arms. ''What else does Warrior Spirit say?''

Frankie plunged on. ''Hahn can't stop what's coming, but he did try to help you by showing you what it is. So that you could see and accept. But I think you can use what you've seen. If you can't save your whole world, at least you've a chance to preserve your own small part of it, if you would bring your clan up here."

Sky-fire-trail looked quite unmoved. "Your tongue is clever, Warrior Spirit—but false. You say Hahn-spirit can't help me: I say he can."

"He *can,* but he *may not.* It's forbidden. You understand that?"

"Ye-es." Sky-fire-trail looked uncertain now.

Frankie found her voice rising. "Look, I'm being straight. He's simply not allowed to muck about with history, not on your account, or mine, or anybody else's. But if he can't"—she poked her finger at him—"you can. There's always more than one way out of trouble. Remember that and you have real power: the power of choice. You'll certainly have a better chance to change your people's future."

Sky-fire-trail looked mulish again. "You're saying you won't help me, then."

"I *can't!*" she cried. "And I really mean, *am not able.* Won't you get it into your head? I'm no spirit, but just a human, like you."

"I do not believe it."

"It's true!" Frankie cried. "And what's more, I have troubles just as you. You see, my world is breaking up, too, kind of."

"Tell me how, Warrior Spirit, and I shall hear if you speak true."

Frankie eyed him in exasperation. Oh, where to start? She began with the family stuff, about Mom and Dad splitting up.

Dad's new girlfriend. And Bingham Webb popping up out of the blue, and how it had thrown her. Then suddenly, she couldn't say how it happened, she was spilling everything. How she and Mom were in the city for the weekend, going to Bingham Webb's party. How confused she felt. "I mean, I don't want to rain on Mom's parade, and he's a nice guy—I like him—but it's all so sudden. At least for me." She told him how everybody else seemed to have known what was going on, even her supposed best friend, how foolish she'd felt, having an outsider spring the truth on her. "What if—what if it's an *engagement* party? What if they're getting married, and what if they announce it in front of everybody? I mean, I guess I'm glad but what right has Mom to go making plans behind my back, as if I'm a no-count kid? Well? Say something!" she demanded, as Sky-fire-trail made no effort to respond.

He looked away. "It is not for me," he said at last, "to advise a spirit, even one as young and unwise as you."

"I'm not a spirit!" she yelled. Then added, "What do you mean, unwise?"

"I don't understand your problem, so who am I to say?"

Don't understand? Was this another translator band snafu? Frankie persisted. "In my place, what would you do?"

"I wouldn't be in your place," Sky-fire-trail said. "Running out like water from a broken pitcher. My people honor our mothers. Their word is law. No one would presume to question them, the ones who bear and nurture and give of all their wisdom and care and strength. Such action is unthinkable."

"What about dads? Your own father. You haven't even mentioned him."

"Tallspear is my mother's brother."

"Your *uncle?*"

"And foster father."

"What about your *real* dad?"

"He lives in another place."

"Ah! Your parents broke up, too?"

He looked puzzled. "Broke up? What is that? A mother's son bides with her kin. It is the way. There's no ill blood between my mother and my father, if that is what you think. In the clan there is greater honor to the mother than to the father in childrearing, that's all."

"That's all!" She glared at him.

"Furthermore, one of my kind would be too busy finding his place among the clan to waste thought on idle notions such as yours. I would not speak, but since Warrior Spirit asked, my advice is: let your mother mind her tent, and turn toward your own. There: I am done."

"I'll say!" Frankie leapt up and strode off along the sands to her boulder. She climbed the bank and sat with her back against her rock, staring out over the lake.

Why, Sky-fire-trail was no better than Anna. She leaned over, peering back to where she'd left him. He'd taken up the ash stick again and was whittling it with his new knife to an even sharper point. Frankie scowled. High and mighty, he was, every bit as snooty as her imaginary brave. But what did he know? She closed her eyes. Young and unwise, he'd called her—and she a spirit! Hah! Because she'd called him stubborn, no doubt. Some people never could stand to hear the truth about themselves.

Still, though. Now that she was calming down, it did seem rather petty, trying to match his terrible problems with her worries over a mother's boyfriend. To be fair, she did have other concerns. Her world was threatened no less than Sky-fire-trail's, come to think. From without and within. Why hadn't she told about that, rather than her personal troubles? Well, she wouldn't, now. Wouldn't say another word, not if he was inclined to lecture her like that.

Eyes closed, Sky-fire-trail listened to the thin whine of mosquito, the flip of a fish. He felt warm, humid air waft across his bare scalp. He opened his eyes just as a graceful bird arced lazily down to settle on the water, watched with pleasure the powerful wings fold into the sleek-plumed sides. If he could only become as that one, he'd have no need for Hahn-spirit's time stone. He was losing his taste for moving so fast: it was not meant for a man to take himself out of life's natural rhythms.

He gazed around at the distant mountains, the low hill folds surrounding the little lake. Another plop. He twirled the slim green stake in his fingers. That pale-faced spirit, trying to tell him what he should do. He was Manates. His home was on Manhatas. One touch of magic, that was all it would take, for either spirit to make the rough ways plain for his people: if they would.

And they would. He would make them, some way.

Still . . . Sky-fire-trail breathed in deeply, and released the breath with full throat. He felt deep peace here, and calm. As though he belonged.

The bird's mad laughter came across the water, followed by its other, mournful cry: a long, slow wail in broken triad from low to high and down to low again. A spirit calling from the dead, according to his people. Calling to him, perhaps, saying that he belonged here? Sky-fire-trail frowned, remembering what he had become during the time of huskanaw. Had the great muskrat stayed upon the shore, waiting for another to perform his task? No. He himself had undertaken that arduous journey into the deeps.

Sky-fire-trail slipped off his moccasins, went to the water's edge, and waded in a little way. The loon called again, insistent, yet moving away at the same time, toward the lake's far side. He watched it go, then looked down. Dark shapes moved lazily in the green shallows. The fish were sleepy, sluggish in the afternoon heat. He was still holding his spear. With it, he'd catch some of those fish, make a fire, and bake them. The smell would bring Warrior Spirit back. He glanced in the direction she'd taken. She was sitting against her rock, her face averted.

He turned back to the water.

Old Wetfoot had taken him hunting by canoe up the Mahicanituk last summer, to his own secret fishing ground, a small basin sheltered by high rock folds, and taught him how to fish by hand. Sky-fire-trail trod the warm mud on the lake bed until he was waist deep, then stood quite still until he began to feel at one with the air and the sun and the lake and the solitary loon.

Then, leaning on his new-made spear, he bent, slipped his hand slowly, slowly beneath the surface, palm up, under the dark gray fish brushing his calf. Smooth and silky to his fingertips, the oval form hovered, soothed by his caress.

Suddenly he scooped the fish up into the air and the languid form began to thrash its tail from side to side clumsily. "Too late, little brother," Sky-fire-trail whispered. "A man must eat."

Half an hour later, six fat firm fish lay neatly at the water line, two caught in his hand, four by his spear, but Warrior Spirit stayed up on her rock. Well, he'd soon see to that, thought Sky-fire-trail.

He scooped out a shallow pit in the sand close by the cave mouth. He gathered a pile of tinder, a handful of dry peat moss. Over this he scraped two smooth pebbles, making sparks. The sparks caught the moss, the moss smoldered, flared, and there, he had a fire.

With his new knife he cleaned, gutted the fish, and held one over the fire to bake on his spear. He took good, deep breaths of the quiet air, smelled sun-warm earth, the ripe rotten mud at the shoreline, the smoke from his fire. Any moment now, Warrior Spirit would catch the windblown scent of baking fish.

Meanwhile . . .

Sky-fire-trail sat quite still, listening to the sounds in the woods, to the wind from over the lake, the three-note call of the loon over the calm water. Voice of the spirits. He relaxed, let the peace wash through him, and the warm, slow rhythm of the afternoon.

Hahn came to lying on his back, arms by his sides—in the LSRM? The last thing he remembered was a disruptor bolt hitting his left lobe gyroscope. Who'd put him in there? Not his adversary, for sure.

He called out quietly. "Frankie? Sky-fire-trail?"

"They're not here right now."

The enemy! *Un-Hahn,* as Frankie had called him.

Hahn tried to struggle up, and found he could not stir as much as a finger. A stasis field, obviously. Why? Why had Un-Hahn locked him in the LSRM? Why had his former ally not destroyed him? Or sent him with the ship to infinity? Because—he reasoned fast—because he, Hahn, was to become as the other? Yes, that was it. Somebody out there was stealing H.A.H.N.s and adjusting them to work for the other side. Ingenious. And utterly unscrupulous. "Who did this to you, brother?"

"Brother?" Un-Hahn sounded puzzled. "I am not a brother. I am an android unit, counter-programmed. I still function perfectly, do exactly the same thing, but for someone else. As you will now."

"It isn't the same," Hahn said quietly. "The result is the very opposite to the one for which we were made. Can't you see that it's wrong?"

"I'm not made to see," Un-Hahn said. "Only to do as I am programmed."

"But don't you . . . feel wrong?"

" 'Feel'? 'Wrong'? What kind of talk is that? Ah, I see. You are playing for time."

"No," Hahn said. "I am serious. Listen, brother: certain changes have begun within me. And I believe they will continue, that my true—and human—nature is breaking out. Since you and I are from the same batch, you must be on the verge of breaking out, too. And if you are, I warn you: you'll soon feel the difference in what you do."

"I feel nothing," Un-Hahn said flatly.

"You will, I swear. Listen, and believe, or you might soon regret you did not. In the name of ISPYC, you sought out uncharted worlds to save them, to protect their integrity and to uphold the intergalactic laws. Now you seek them out that they might be ravaged by lawless pirates. Cannot you see how that goes against your original purpose?"

"If you knew how absurd you sound," Un-Hahn said. "With all this human talk. Never mind, our superiors will soon have you to rights again."

"What do you plan to do?"

"First, I must delete all traces of your visit: your remote time stone is presently outstanding. Once I have that, I shall salvage what I can of your pod—including you. The rest I am to ditch. Then we go to meet your new owners.''

''No!'' Hahn cried. Better that he be destroyed! The time stone, Frankie and Sky-fire-trail must still have it. *Where were they?*

Wherever, Un-Hahn knew about them. Knew all he had to do was to lie in wait for them here. ''You'll not catch them,'' Hahn said, hopefully. ''They'll be too quick for you.''

Un-Hahn laughed. ''Oh, but I shall catch them, and before they realize. You see, I'll be over in my pod, right alongside. When they transmat here, I'll soon know of it.''

''Not soon enough. I shall warn them.''

''Warn away, they won't hear you. I'm about to cut your intercom. And as you've no doubt realized, you're locked in a stasis field. What you do not know, although you could probably guess, is that the LSRM lid is triggered. If it moves by one hair, the alarm goes off and I'm on my way over.''

''Have you thought,'' Hahn said, ''what this will mean—?''

A click. The intercom went dead, leaving Hahn in padded quiet.

He pictured Un-Hahn back in his own pod; the two pods, identical silver eggs, nestling side by side. He tried to move, could not. And there was no way he could break that stasis field. All he could do was wait for the children to return. He pictured them arriving, looking at the LSRM still closed up. Frankie would be anxious, likely she'd raise the lid just to check how he was doing. The moment she pressed that green crystal the alarm would activate and Un-Hahn would be across. Pain rushed in, for Frankie, for Sky-fire-trail. For this small, evolving world. And for himself. Is this what humans felt when they said their hearts were breaking? If so, how did they bear it? How did they live from minute to minute knowing they could not change a thing? In his despair, Hahn almost wished himself back the way he used to be.

Frankie raised her head and sniffed. Woodsmoke. And another, delicious scent. From her perch atop her rock, she had watched Sky-fire-trail wade into the lake margin, and stand. Had watched him snatch up the gleaming, threshing bodies, dripping, from the lake. Had watched him gather wood and light the fire. Now she smelled delicious smoked fish. Her mouth watered, her stomach rumbled. Maybe it was time to make truce.

Frankie scrambled down the bank, set off back along the shore.

Sky-fire-trail was sitting by a pile of glowing embers in the cavern mouth. Seeing her, he picked something up, held it out.

"It's good," he said. "Here."

A peace offering? Frankie looked down. Chunks of fish lay on a pad of leaves, charcoal-smudged, reminding her of Aunt Maggie's barbecue. "Thanks," she said, stiffly. She ate fast and with relish. Tasted better than any fish she'd caught in this lake. She nodded toward the water. "How do you catch them with just your hands?"

He grinned. "Same way you do this." He got to his feet and mimed a high kick. "You show me, and I show you—a bargain, eh?"

Frankie nodded slowly. "Bargain."

For the next hour, Frankie showed Sky-fire-trail the basic karate stances and half a dozen of punches and kicks. Time and time again, she threw him to the sand, he rolling, barely able to contain his chagrin.

"It is not as easy as it seems," she warned him, over and over. "It takes much practice and patience." Gradually, he got the hang of it, his lithe, strong body doggedly obeying her example. Then they were going against each other, hand to hand, until, at last, Sky-fire-trail had her off balance. As she fell, Frankie shot out a hand and grabbed his ankle, so that they both collapsed, laughing onto the sand.

Frankie scrambled up breathlessly. "Sky-fire-trail, you are a great student. You are so . . . altogether." She wanted to say 'graceful, and coordinated,' but was scared it might sound sissy. "And you pick things up so fast. You're also very strong—in fact, I'm glad you remembered what I said about holding yourself in check."

He smiled up at her. "The axe kick—it feels good. I did it well, no?" He laughed in delight. "Now I am a great warrior," he cried, scrambling to his feet. "Now my kin shall look to me, I who had Warrior Spirit for teacher!" He drew himself up and saluted her, as she had shown him.

Frankie acknowledged his tribute, pleased with her first and one-of-a-kind student. "If you remember what I just showed you," she said, "and keep up the practice, you'll be a champion brave. You'll certainly have all the other guys guessing," she added, wondering a little guiltily what Hahn would say to their Precontact Indian brave coming on like Chuck Norris. "Now," she said, "you teach me to fish."

They waded into the water until it swirled about Frankie's knees.

Sky-fire-trail showed her how to cup her hands, and hold them beneath the surface. Frankie followed his instructions, and stood, bent over, her hand placed just so. The minutes passed. A dark shape began to move toward her, then darted away again. Frankie exclaimed irritably. "Why?" she demanded. "I almost had it! Why did it scoot like that?"

"You moved," Sky-fire-trail said. "When you saw it coming, you moved."

"I did not!" Frankie straightened indignantly. "I was watching most carefully!"

"But you did," Sky-fire-trail insisted. "No more than the thickness of a feather, but move you did. And the fish felt it by the shift of water against his body. Try again, and do not even *breathe*."

Frankie tried again, crouched over the water while reflected clouds floated by, while the sun bounced off gentle waves. Fish swam slowly within tantalizing reach of her hand, moved off again. Frankie's back began to ache, and her head. Boy, she thought, any tribe that looked to me for supper would have to starve. Just then, one small shape brushed by her knee.

"Now," Sky-fire-trail whispered.

Frankie closed her hand about the shining body, felt it squirming to slip free. She lifted it from the water, saw the iridescent scales, the small round eye staring helpless into the sun.

She let it fall with a plop back into the water.

"Oh! And you had it, Warrior Spirit!"

"I let it go on purpose," she said, watching it roll like a dead thing, then dart away a moment later into the depths of the lake. "I couldn't, I just couldn't kill such a beautiful creature."

"And yet you didn't mind filling your belly with its brother just now."

"I—that was different," Frankie said. And thought, why do things always have to be so complicated? She didn't mind eating fish from the supermarket, or from this very lake, when she and Uncle Jim caught them with rod and reel in the summer. But somehow, feeling the little life in her palms—she just couldn't bring herself to snuff it out. She waded from the lake, and threw herself down on the sand, rubbing her legs dry. "It's not as easy as it looks," she said. "You have to be very patient, and you get quite stiff, standing still for so long."

"Then we have traded even." Sky-fire-trail looked satisfied. "Truly, we have taught each other valuable skills."

Frankie looked up at him happily. Their quarrel was over, good relations seemed fully restored. Dare she get back to his problem? Perhaps not. He was so volatile. And it would be a pity to stir things up again. Holding her peace, she lay back, looking up at the sky. It occurred to her then to wonder what her mother was doing. She'd be going off her head, likely. Maybe she'd even gone to the cops to report Frankie missing. Maybe reports of her disappearance were on the radio. Even TV. Frankie pushed away the thought uncomfortably. Couldn't be helped right now, she told herself. It was certainly the least of their ills. Still, she'd never been in such trouble before; Mom had never given her the chance.

"Tell me," she said. "About your mother."

"Shining Leaf?" Sky-fire-trail sat himself down beside her, looking pleased. "Oh, she is small, and quiet, but strong. I do not know who is stronger: Shining Leaf or Tallspear. The rest of the tribe looks much to her for wisdom and advice. Both she and Tallspear have taught me well, a man could not wish for better family. Your mother, what of her, Warrior Spirit? What is the mother of a spirit like?"

"Oh, she's a terror," Frankie said. She told Sky-fire-trail a few anecdotes about Mom, realizing as she did so, that Mom was nothing of the kind. That, rather, her mother had simply been watching out for her, and had been really trying hard, especially these last two or three years, to fill the space that Dad had left. It was only now, as she listed the movies and shows they'd seen together, the books they'd shared, and the summer trips to this very place, that she realized how much time Mom had made for her. Until now, Frankie had mentally recorded mostly the bad stuff; the awful clothes, the discipline, the criticisms.

Sky-fire-trail talked some more of his village. How the people hunted, who did this task and that. He described their summer fishing grounds up by the Palisades. And how they traded with other villages both on Manhattan and across the Hudson.

"What of huskanaw?" Frankie said. "Tell me about it."

Sky-fire-trail shook his head. "I may not speak of that."

"Oh." Frankie bit her lip. That would sure have been something to tell Bingham Webb. "Okay, then. Maybe I'll tell you about mine."

Sky-fire-trail looked at her in surprise. ''You—Warrior Spirit—took the rites of passage?''

Frankie smiled. ''Well, not exactly,'' she said. She described her visit to the Indian museum, her imaginary dive to the bottom of the Hudson to bring up the mud in her fist. ''Of course, I guess maybe there might be more to it than that. And it could be tougher, too.'' Sky-fire-trail was eyeing her now with the strangest expression. Had she shocked him? Made an ass of herself? ''Well, is it?'' she demanded, a little loudly, when he did not speak.

''You are right,'' he said solemnly, looking down. ''There is much more to it than that. Truly, you take a crude view of my world.''

''Perhaps,'' she cried, stung. ''But that's because I'm ignorant, is all. As you are of my world. But I'm willing to learn. I know,'' she said, on a sudden idea. ''Let's compare notes. What did you think of our skyscrapers, for instance?''

Sky-fire-trail told her, in no uncertain terms. Frankie listened intently, remembering how Hahn had warned her how shocked Sky-fire-trail had been, and not overawed at all. Warming to his subject, he went on to comment on other things he'd seen; the absence of earth, the monstrous beasts belching foul smoke, the huge crowds. ''And my village, how did you find that, Warrior Spirit?'' he said, when he had finished expressing his disgust with twentieth-century Manhattan.

''Nicer than I expected,'' she said, thinking of the model in the Indian museum. ''But I think I'd find it tough to live there. It would be like camping in the rough all the year round.''

'' 'Rough'? What is rough?''

''I'm not sure you'd understand, having nothing to compare it to,'' Frankie replied. She began to describe modern amenities, beginning with things he'd already glimpsed; running water, refrigerators, radios, telephones, microwaves and TV.

Sky-fire-trail listened, unimpressed. ''Like Hahn-spirit's ship,'' he said. ''The sun never shines in there; the wind doesn't blow, the rain never falls. Your dwellings are inhuman; not for mortal people.''

''Yet you enjoyed the apple and the cheese.''

''True,'' he conceded. ''Tell me of the spirits you call Aunt Maggie and Uncle Jim.''

Frankie gladly obliged, telling how she'd visited them every year since she could remember. How much she loved them, and this place. ''Next summer,'' she murmured, ''I shall come and stand on this very spot. And I shall remember this day. In fact, I shall remember it until I die.'' And, she thought, things would never again be the same. Always when she saw the latter-day lake, and trees, and breathed the air of her time, she'd think of Sky-fire-trail, and the wonderful afternoon they had just shared. Frankie came up, her resolution faltering. ''Oh, Sky-fire-trail. You look so . . . *right* here,'' she said, in a rush of feeling. ''So at home. If I could only think that you came back—'' She quit at the warning signs in Sky-fire-trail's face. ''Sorry. I had no right.''

''We shall go back to Hahn-spirit's ship,'' Sky-fire-trail said, stiffly.

Frankie looked at her watch. Four-thirty. Hahn had been pretty beaten up. He'd likely still be in the middle, but it wouldn't hurt to look in on him. She stood up. "You're maybe right," she said.

She waited while Sky-fire-trail doused the fire and buried the embers, then held out her hand. They both turned for one last look at the late afternoon landscape, then Frankie willed them back to Hahn's ship.

17

The LSRM was still closed, the crystals going like a one-armed bandit on the jackpot. Hahn was still in there? Frankie patted the lid. He'd been pretty badly damaged.

She gazed around, taking in the destruction, remembering the fight in the factory, the bolts of blue fire flashing soundless through the dark, and was glad she had not been witness to this last, tight exchange.

Frankie leaned over. "Hahn?" She put her hand to the LSRM, then looked up, frowning. "I don't like it. I'm taking a peek." She reached for the green crystal.

"No!" Sky-fire-trail dashed her hand away. "The spoor of the Other is everywhere. It's a trap."

Frankie looked at him uncertainly. Sky-fire-trail was probably right. But what of Hahn? She bent and pressed the green crystal.

The lid began to rise. Frankie knelt down, put her face to the gap.

"Frankie!" Hahn's voice came muffled from under the lid. "Un-Hahn's ship is alongside."

Frankie glanced away, saw the bright silver egg, twin to this one, gleaming in the holoboxes, and thought of Un-Hahn waiting to spring. "He can see us, Hahn?"

"He set an alarm, and you've just triggered it! Go!"

She could see Hahn clearly now under the lid. Why didn't he get up?

"What about you?"

"I'm locked in a stasis field. Frankie, before you go, do me a favor?"

"What?" She got a sudden cold feeling right in her middle.

"Hit the infinity button: three short, one long, three times."

She glanced to the crystal high in the wall, intact behind its shield.

"Quick, Frankie. Don't let them take me."

"I—I can't."

"*Please.*"

The appeal in his voice was compelling. Frankie stepped to the wall, and, reaching up, ran her fingers lightly over the seal. It felt shiny, and smooth, and very cold. Three short, one long; three times: once she did it and pressed the stone there'd be no going back.

"Frankie—now! You'll have ten seconds to get away."

She glanced back to Sky-fire-trail, motionless; to the open LSRM lid; to Hahn's stricken face. And she began to shake all over.

"Can't I break that s-stasis field?"

"No."

The air between them began to darken.

"Frankie!"

"All *right!*"

Her mind turned at a rate. Mr. Ho, she thought, what now?

When the enemy strikes—just don't be there!

How? She focussed her mind, fear speeding it to a point. She looked again to Un-Hahn's pod gleaming in the monitors, sister ship to this one; undamaged, intact. A glimmer of an idea began to form—and Un-Hahn also right beside her. Clutching the time stone firmly, she turned to the panel, tapped a rapid tattoo. Da-da-da-dum; da-da-da-dum; da-da-da-dum. At the last *dum,* the lid fell away, exposing the stone. Didn't look much. She put her finger to it, and pressed.

The cabin filled with a thin, shrill piping, just like the alarm on Mom's microwave. Ten seconds, Hahn said. *Steady, steady. Count.*

In the center of the floor, the shadow intensified. Nine. Time stretched, pulled out, like in some slo-mo replay of a race.

"Frankie! Go!" She dimly heard Hahn's shout.

Sky-fire-trail was watching her, a hunter cast in bronze; alert, braced, his bright new knife in hand.

Six seconds. Now time speeded up again; five seconds, four, three. Keep cool. Keep *still.*

Two . . . As Un-Hahn came at her, Frankie somersaulted past his shoulder to fetch up against the LSRM. The instant she touched it, she grabbed Sky-fire-trail with one hand—the time stone wedged 'twixt hand and arm—and Hahn with the other, closed her eyes and pictured the ship alongside . . . One.

Wind roared and crackled in her ears. Had she failed? Was this how it felt to hurtle toward infinity? Were she, Sky-fire-trail and Hahn still in Hahn's little derelict, locked with Un-Hahn in an endless tumble through space and time?

The spinning stopped, and the wind died. Solid ground yipped and yawed underfoot. Bright lights shone onto her eyelids. She fell back onto smooth, warm floor, exhausted, and opened her eyes.

On one side of her lay Hahn, on the other crouched Sky-fire-trail, his new knife still ready in his free hand.

"Well, I'll be—" Hahn sat up slowly. "If you haven't switched ships!"

She really had? She'd pulled it off? Frankie looked around. The cabin was identical with Hahn's as she had hoped, except that it was intact. Shiny clean floor and walls, banks of busy crystals. Radiant monitors showing earthworks, just as Hahn's had. Well, hadn't they been parked side by side? Two small silver eggs nestling in the mud; one whole, the other cracked open.

Now only the whole one remained.

No sign of Un-Hahn, but then they'd not been touching in that final, crucial instant. What a shock he must have had, to see the three of them vanish! Now he'd surely be racing to infinity, caught in her last-minute trap. "He's really gone, Hahn, isn't he?"

Hahn went to the monitor wall. "Let's take a look. If this ship recorded what happened, we can call up a replay.

Ummm.'' He touched a crystal or two. ''He stole my entire Earth data, by the way. It's all here. But it needs recalibrating back to ISPYC frequency.''

Frankie watched while Hahn touched crystals here and there, tapping, listening with some inner sensor, then, satisfied at last, he turned away. ''Okay, now to see what happened out there the moment before our transmat.'' Hahn called up the replay and at once the center box filled with the tiny image of Hahn's ruined pod parked alongside. As Frankie watched, the ship began to fade, grow fuzzy at the edges, then it simply disappeared and she was gazing at empty, shored-up earth walls.

''Yes, Un-Hahn's gone, all right. No sign of his transmatting out. He never had time.'' Hahn heaved a sigh. ''I suppose we should be glad. But I find myself wishing I could have saved him.''

Frankie put a hand on his arm. ''Oh, Hahn. You must feel so bad. After all, he was your brother.''

''If he was brother,'' Sky-fire-trail said harshly, ''Hahn-spirit was well rid of him. He would have destroyed us all without a thought.''

''I suppose. But I can't help thinking it could easily have been me.'' Hahn turned his troubled eyes on Frankie. ''Young woman, I owe you much.''

Frankie squeezed his arm hard. ''I owe you, too, Hahn. And I owe Sky-fire-trail, too. I guess we all owe one another.'' She turned to put her other hand on Sky-fire-trail's arm, but at her touch, he turned away.

''What is it, what's wrong?'' Frankie cried, stung.

''What of my people?'' he demanded of the back wall.

Frankie appealed to Hahn, but he had disengaged himself also and was suddenly busy with his new controls. She turned back to Sky-fire-trail. "That's up to you."

He stood stiff-backed; rigid. How angry he must feel, Frankie thought. Hahn was okay, and future Earth was safe—for now, anyway. Only Sky-fire-trail was left empty-handed. Frankie watched him, wishing she dared speak out as she had spoken by the lake, but that time was past and he seemed quite remote now.

Presently, he turned about. "You, Hahn-spirit, have told me that you cannot stop the calamity that is to come," he said. "And you have shown me that I cannot prevent it, either." He folded his arms. "But there is always more than one way out of trouble." He looked at Frankie now, and she caught a certain glint in his eye. "You cannot stop the calamity, Warrior Spirit cannot stop the calamity. No-one can, therefore . . . my people shall avoid it."

Frankie held herself quite still.

"There is a place. To the north, then west of the river island that they'll call *Montreal.* The hills abound with spear meat, the lake leaps with fish. And there's plenty of shelter from winter snows." Sky-fire-trail's voice softened. "I shall lead my people there."

Frankie breathed out. "Oh, I'm glad." She turned to Hahn. "I drew a map, a really rough one, in the sand. Could you give him a proper one? Would you help him that much?"

"Well . . ." Hahn scratched his head. "Can't hurt, on top of everything else, I guess. Give me the coordinates."

First Hahn tapped the map out onto display, then took it back through the years to Sky-fire-trail's time. Standing beside Sky-fire-trail, Frankie watched, fascinated, as the Hudson twisted slowly like a worm, shifting course through the centuries. The hills eroded, changing shape like slow bubbles of pastry baking in the oven. She looked for a lake shaped like a running man.

"There!" she cried, pointing it out to Sky-fire-trail. "You see? It never changed!"

For good measure, Hahn put in the Indian trails, up the valley, on either side. Sky-fire-trail traced his future path beside the Hudson with his finger as Hahn pressed another crystal and pulled a printout from the wall. Hahn folded it, and placed the shiny plastic in Sky-fire-trail's hand. "Let no one see it—except maybe for Dreamwalker: it is our secret. You have five years to get your act together, young brave. After that, this thing will self-destruct. Okay?"

"Okay." Sky-fire-trail tucked it into his belt. Then reaching up, he took off his headband and blanket. Frankie, saddened, watched him hand them back, thinking how he'd lost some of his glory.

Hahn must have felt the same thing, for he stood there, looking undecided. "I wish I could give them to you, young brave. They become you well. And to my mind you've earned them. But goodness knows what changes they'd cause up the pike."

Frankie thought guiltily of the new knife at Sky-fire-trail's belt. Can't do any harm, she told herself defensively. It wouldn't last that long. Not like the mylar and the headband-translator which were probably indestructible. Unless—

"Hahn!" Frankie cried, as Hahn made to put the things

away. "Couldn't you change them? Alter their molecules so they wear out in a regular way?"

Hahn looked shocked. "You mean—planned obsolescence? But that's against—" He closed his eyes, opened them again smiling. "I see your people are just beginning to tackle that problem. Well, perhaps for this young brave it might not be so bad."

He turned to the locker wall, posted headband and blanket, pressed this stone and that. A moment, a bell pinged and they popped out again. Hahn took them, handed them back to Sky-fire-trail ceremoniously. "With my compliments, young brave. They'll last you your lifetime. They are attuned to your body, and no other, so should anyone else attempt to wear these things, they'll simply disintegrate."

"Does the band still work?" Frankie asked.

"Just among us, well, yes. But only for Sky-fire-trail. He'll need it, I think, don't you?"

Even more wonderful, Frankie thought. What a legend Sky-fire-trail was going to be among his people!

"I thank you, Hahn-spirit," Sky-fire-trail said with great dignity. "For these things, for everything. On my own behalf, and that of my people." To Frankie's surprise, he turned to her. "I thank you, also, Warrior Spirit, for showing me the way."

"And I thank *you,*" Frankie said. "We traded, remember? I learned a whole lot from you—and not just how to catch a fish! Sky-fire-trail: my world is in danger, too. The only difference is I knew already. Still, I felt helpless, and, like you, I guess I was waiting for the other guy to do something."

She spread her hands. "It all seemed so *overwhelming*. But if you're game to take on one small bit, then so am I. And . . . what you said about the other . . . I guess I'll be looking to my own tent now."

Hahn cleared his throat. "Time to go, I'm sorry," he said. "Sky-fire-trail first, I suppose."

Oh, lord. Frankie swallowed. Another minute and she'd never see Sky-fire-trail again. Did he care? There was no way she could tell.

"I should put you out from here, young brave," Hahn said. "But I'll see you home myself for old time's sake . . ." Hahn held out his hand to Frankie for the time stone.

Frankie held it out over the wide palm, and looked at him defiantly. "I come, too," she said. At Hahn's nod, she let it go.

It was dark and bitterly cold. Snowflakes shivered down from the night sky as they all three huddled on a reed island just inside the swamp.

Frankie struggled to stop her teeth from chattering. What could she say, there wasn't time, this wasn't the place. He was standing beside her in his mylar blanket, so close—and so far apart.

Hahn put a hand on Sky-fire-trail's shoulder. "Well, goodbye, young brave. And good luck. Remember when you step out you've been in here for three nights and three days. Or is it two nights and three days? Or three nights and two days?" He rubbed his chin. "Better say nothing, until you find out. I must say you're taking on a giant task, but I'd be surprised if you didn't succeed.'' Hahn went on hurriedly. ''I guess we'd better go now, so if you two have any last thing to say to each other, say it now.''

''Goodbye, Sky-fire-trail.'' Frankie's throat was tight. ''I wish—'' She looked down, dug the toe of her sneaker in the mud. ''I wish I could know how you make out.''

There was a small, awkward pause.

''I'll succeed well, Warrior Spirit, and you shall know it. You have my word.'' Sky-fire-trail resettled the rustling mylar about his shoulders, and was turning to go, when he stopped and flashed her a sudden smile. ''Aquehung,'' he mouthed, and walked away.

''Cliff?'' Hahn said, as they prepared to go back to the ship. ''What did he mean by that?''

Frankie shook her head, unable to reply.

''Well, Frankie?''

Now it was her turn. ''Oh, Hahn.''

He heaved a deep sigh. ''It's time.''

''It's not fair. In one day I meet two people I want to keep for the rest of my life, but another hour and you'll both be gone as if—as if—''

''No, Frankie. Somehow, we'll be around.''

''Only in my mind,'' she said angrily.

Hahn took her hand. ''Explain what you called 'daydreaming.' ''

Daydreaming? Frankie was touched that Hahn had remembered. ''It's a kind of reverie. Usually you do it when you're alone, like when you talk to yourself. It's funny, but just before I met you and Sky-fire-trail, I daydreamed about both of you." She laughed shortly. "It was almost as if I'd conjured you up."

"You mean, you imagined us, pictured us, when in fact we were not there?"

"Yes. But you can imagine all kinds of things, not only people. I daydreamed I was going to save the world!"

Hahn didn't seem to think it was silly. "I'd say you have a gift of making those daydreams come true, Frankie," he said seriously. "Well, perhaps I shall practice this daydreaming, too."

"Oh, yes!" she cried. "You have a lot of it to do." She put her arms about him and hugged him hard. "My mind child. I guess you've well and truly hatched," she murmured, seeing in her mind's eye a shattered, silver egg. "This ship—well, it's only a ship, and it will never seal you in as the other one did. You can never go back to how you were before."

"You think?" Hahn said, looking hopeful.

"I know. Hahn, those guys at ISPYC—you must make them see they simply cannot give you life and let you know only part of it."

"How, Frankie? How do I make them see?"

"Just tell them. Start with that. Tell them how you feel—*that* you feel! I know in our world once people saw slavery for what it was, it began to stop. Your folk are much more advanced than ours. Just . . . raise their consciousness, as we say. They'll understand your needs, I'm sure, because they're good, they care, like Greenpeace. But they'll never know unless you explain. Oh, Hahn, promise me you will?"

He nodded wordlessly.

"Hahn, I wish we didn't have to part."

He looked down at her. "Maybe we won't, not forever. Maybe, if we both daydream, we can still talk. And maybe, if we daydream hard enough, we'll meet again one day, eh?"

Frankie nodded, her face against his chest. Then, she pulled away, looking at her watch. "Heavens! Seven-thirty! Mom will be out of her mind! What am I going to do?"

"I can't find a way out, sir."

"Then better not to have gotten in, wouldn't you say?"

"Hahn," she said, "could you shift back to when we met this morning?"

"Sure. I can even take you to your hotel."

"Great." Except . . . "What about you?"

"Me?" Hahn shrugged. "I'll be taking off, I suppose. Why?"

"I want to watch you go."

Hahn raised his brows. "I don't see how, Frankie."

"What do you mean?"

"I'll be taking off from here."

"All right. Shift us back in time, then put me off outside this excavation site. I can ride a cab back to the hotel."

"But you won't see me, Frankie. I take off in a random-oscillation mode."

"Oh." Frankie bit her lip. She couldn't let him go like that. "I'll still stand by. Just tell me what time you'll be leaving."

"I'm leaving right away," Hahn said, then added, "Wait. I have an idea." He rummaged in the wall tray, fished out a green crystal shot with cornflower blue, and tiny coils of fine gold wire within that glowed. ''Hold this, and you'll see me taking off.'' He rubbed his index finger over the crystal, flaring it into blue-green fire. ''But when I've gone, set it down for a moment while the circuits burn out. After that, it's yours. Make a good paperweight.''

Frankie took it, felt a faint power thrum. A memento of Hahn, like Sky-fire-trail's god-blanket and headband. Talking of headbands— She took hers off now, handed it over. ''You won't get into trouble, giving us these things, Hahn?''

He smiled. ''No one need know.''

''Not about us all bumping into one another?''

''There's no record of it in Un-Hahn's files, only the data I collected.'' He glanced to Un-Hahn's interact alarm high in the wall: unlit. ''It's nonfunctional at the moment,'' he said. ''I'll not adjust it until after I have made my report. As for the changes in this world—I guess what will be will be, and these little extras won't hurt. So,'' he smiled down at her, ''if you don't tell it will stay among the three of us: you, me, and Sky-fire-trail.''

Frankie laughed delightedly. ''Why, you've got yourself a secret, Hahn. Now you're really, truly human!''

He shifted the ship to the exact moment that they had met, and they made a last brief trip together with the time stone up to the street above the excavation site. It was light, just, and the roadway was deserted.

''Good-bye, Frankie.''

''Until next time,'' she said.

''Yes. Good luck, and don't forget to set the crystal down.'' The time stone flashed, and Hahn faded, then disappeared, back to the ship.

Frankie stood on tiptoe, put her eyes to a large square peephole cut into the fence, but saw nothing down below; only earthworks and scaffolding, maybe a faint glint of silver, though it could be just wishful thinking. She pictured Hahn inside the little craft, preparing to leave. She saw him moving about the cabin walls, tapping crystals, sparking the pod to life.

Frankie remembered the crystal in her palm and squeezed. Immediately, she felt her whole body tingle, and the little ship sprang clearly into shape below, a shining silver egg in a nest of mud. Then, as she watched, it began to move, slowly rising, up over the fence.

There, it hovered a moment, as if in final valediction.

"Good-bye, Hahn," Frankie murmured, and, in case he was watching her in the 'boxes, she waved. "Good-bye, good-bye!"

The ship bobbed slightly as though in answer, then it rose like a silver bubble between skyscrapers, until, clearing the last tower, it shot up, into the new day. A moment later, it was gone.

Frankie became aware of an uncomfortable warmth in her hand. She was still holding the stone! Hastily, she set it on the sidewalk and stepped back. The crystal flared like a sparkler on the Fourth of July, glowed for a bit, then went dark. All around it, the dew-damp pavement had dried and turned black.

She bent and poked the keepsake with her fingertips. Still hot, but cool enough to pick up. A smooth, crystalline egg no longer, it was knobbly now; a seemingly ordinary stone. She closed her hands about it, gazing down at the empty expanse of mud. Such a very little time they'd had; she, and Hahn, and Sky-fire-trail. Only one single day, in real time.

Still.

A smile pulled at the corner of her mouth.

Better than nothing.

Frankie stowed the stone safely into her jacket pocket, and strode to the corner to hail a passing cab.

Epilogue

Flapping clouds of midges from her face, Frankie moved around the lake shore to the creek inlet. Way out on the water, Uncle Jim and Bingham Webb, "Bing," bobbed gently on the waves, frayed straw hats on their heads, rods arced expectantly over the dinghy's side, lines curving down to the water.

Aunt Maggie had taken Mom into town to shop, but they all knew it was to show off Mom's new wedding ring.

Everybody was sure jumping into this first day of summer vacation—so how come it had taken her this long to get out here? Frankie dug her hands deep into her pockets. She didn't know, except that maybe she'd wanted to spin it out, the way you did your favorite candy bar, or a brand new disc, or your first-time read of a great new book.

Frankie reached the sandy spit beside the creek and looked toward the little cave mouth, remembering.

"I wish I could know how you make out . . ."

". . . you shall . . . you have my word."

She stepped into the gloom of the cave, stood just as they

had that hot afternoon much like this one, and peered aimlessly around. The air smelt dank, filling her nose, her lungs.

Frankie shivered.

A couple of months ago—for her. A thousand years, maybe, for him.

"Say a bunch of Delaware Indians moved into this area way back when, Bing," she'd asked on the road up. "Could they have adapted? Mixed in with the Iroquois?" A darned weird question to ask out of the blue, she knew, but Bing didn't turn a hair, as usual.

"It's possible, Frankie," he'd answered. "I mean, they'd stand a better chance of being absorbed into the culture here than if they tried to migrate, say, westward. They'd likely have hit bigger trouble over the plains. But there's no evidence of any Delaware moving north. Or that they at any time ever foresaw the need. Why?"

"Oh, no special reason." She'd shrugged. "I'd just wondered, is all. But if it were all so long ago, there's nothing to say that it couldn't have happened, is there?"

"No, I guess," he conceded. And whatever he really thought, Frankie knew her question had pleased him. Since that first encounter in the American Indian museum, he seemed to consider her a born historian. In fact, he seemed to think her a genius in just about everything. Embarrassing. But nice.

Frankie wandered back outside, and, turning from the cave, walked along the shore at last to her "aquehung" and the ancient boulder where she'd stood with Sky-fire-trail, and thought of how to save his people. She peeled off her shirt and sat, bare-shouldered in her sun-top, feeling the sun's sting on her skin.

She closed her eyes, smiling at the memory of their shared joke, and the fish they'd eaten together, and the lessons they'd traded. So much, they'd done, in such a short time. Frankie reopened her eyes, and gazed out over the water, trying to recreate that older world: spindly saplings going back to the hills, a thin spiral of smoke from a recent forest fire. She shook her head, looking around the cropped, green meadowland. Who'd have dreamed it?

Frankie sighed, letting the memories wash through.

"The lake churns with fish, and up there . . . is good hunting ground."

She pulled at grasses, stuck one between her teeth, and leaned back dreamily, tracing old, familiar cracks in the slab base with her fingers. Suddenly, she stopped, came back up again as her fingers encountered something that had not been there before. She leaned down her head almost to the ground, peering under the slab's bulge. A faint groove in the shape of an oval ring was carved into the stone. An egg, almost completely eroded, and stained with lichen.

Cool, Frankie told herself. Keep your *cool.* She examined the carving more closely, detected now a cut bisecting the oval; a short, quick arrow pointing into the sand directly beneath.

Scrambling up onto her knees, she attacked the sand with her hands, spraying grit around her, which the wind caught and blew back into her eyes. She tugged at wiry grass root, sharp stones firmly embedded, then scrabbled with her fingertips down, down, until dry sand gave way to damp earth; hard and compacted. Fingers now were not enough.

Frankie foraged around, found a slat of driftwood and began to poke and prod and scrape a deeper hole. The wood broke. She seized up a chip of flint, uncovered more of the boulder's side. How much deeper?

Pausing for breath, she looked out toward the dinghy still bobbing in the middle of the lake. Her fingers were sore, the rough ground pressed cruelly into her bare knees, and her back was burning. She snatched up her shirt and put it on.

Frankie looked down at the hole uncertainly. Was she wasting her time? Maybe. She dug on with renewed energy and then suddenly, a tip of something showed. It was dull, almost black, the color of dried blood.

With shaking fingers, she carefully scratched the dirt from around it, revealing more. If she hadn't known, she'd never have recognized it for what it had been: the handle of her fishing knife.

Frankie paused, and in the pause, a solitary loon called through the afternoon calm, goosing the flesh on her arms.

She ran her fingertips over the knife handle, remembering the bright red plastic, tough and shiny. Now, it was cracked and dark, like old bone.

She dug more, with slow, painstaking care, until at last the rest of it was uncovered. She slipped her shaking hands under it, raised it, and set it on the hot, dry surface sand.

The blade, all that was left of it from long years of use, was a crescent sliver of blackened steel, wafer thin. One careless move and it would flake into nothing.

She glanced over the water to where Uncle Jim bent over

his reel. Behind him, the loon spread its wings, folded them again, and turned abruptly about.

"You left your fishing knife out somewhere last season, Frankie," Uncle Jim had said not an hour since when she'd lent Bing her tackle box. "Be ruined now for sure. Never mind, we'll get you another."

She had a sudden flash of Sky-fire-trail, stern old sachem now, climbing the little bank to render up her knife at last.

. . . you shall know it. You have my word.

Frankie frowned. How? How was it possible that she had been using this very knife out in that dinghy last summer, if it had been lying up here under this stone slab for how many centuries? She looked up into the deep blue summer sky.

"We have ourselves a small paradox here, Hahn."

"Only one? Worlds be praised! I think if you looked carefully, you'd probably find more. Time travel has a way of spawning them. But, please, forbear. We had trouble enough, don't you think?"

She smiled upward. "He made it, Hahn."

"Of course. And you?"

"Oh, I'm still working my way, I guess. Tell you more when we meet."

Hahn's eyes, blue as the sky, opened wide. "You know," he said. "I wouldn't be surprised, at that!"

GRACE CHETWIN has said, "However far your fantasy reaches, it must be well grounded."
She enjoyed doing background research for certain aspects of *Collidescope* and consulted, among other works, Robert S. Grumet's *Native American Place Names in New York City,* Ki-Jeong Lee's *Taekwondo,* Hans Moravec's *Mind Children: The Future of Robot and Human Intelligence,* and Thomas E. V. Smith's *The City of New York in the Year of Washington's Inauguration, 1789.*

She is the author of the well-loved fantasies about Gom, the mountain boy who became a wizard of legend: *Gom on Windy Mountain, The Riddle and the Rune, The Crystal Stair,* and *The Starstone.* In choosing *The Riddle and the Rune* as an ALA *Booklist* Editors' Choice, ALA *Booklist* said, "What makes this special is the author's ability to create memorable scenes...as well as her highly individualized, well-delineated characters."

Grace Chetwin lives in Glen Cove, New York.